A Little Bit of Ireland

JOHN FINAN

Trafford
PUBLISHING™

Order this book online at www.trafford.com/07-2627
or email orders@trafford.com

Most Trafford titles are also available at major online book retailers.

Note for Librarians: A cataloguing record for this book is available from Library
and Archives Canada at www.collectionscanada.ca/amicus/index-e.html

Printed in Victoria, BC, Canada.

ISBN: 978-1-4251-5826-2

We at Trafford believe that it is the responsibility of us all, as both individuals
and corporations, to make choices that are environmentally and socially sound.
You, in turn, are supporting this responsible conduct each time you purchase a
Trafford book, or make use of our publishing services. To find out how you are
helping, please visit www.trafford.com/responsiblepublishing.html

Our mission is to efficiently provide the world's finest, most comprehensive
book publishing service, enabling every author to experience success.
To find out how to publish your book, your way, and have it available
worldwide, visit us online at www.trafford.com/10510

Trafford
PUBLISHING™

www.trafford.com

North America & international
toll-free: 1 888 232 4444 (USA & Canada)
phone: 250 383 6864 ♦ fax: 250 383 6804
email: info@trafford.com

The United Kingdom & Europe
phone: +44 (0)1865 722 113 ♦ local rate: 0845 230 9601
facsimile: +44 (0)1865 722 868 ♦ email: info.uk@trafford.com

10 9 8 7 6 5 4 3

Acknowledgements

I WISH TO ACKNOWLEDGE the help of the following people, in compiling this book, "A Little Bit of Ireland".

Maureen Cronin nee Gallagher, Cloonfane, for her photographs.

Mrs. Brennan Cloonlyon, for her help with the story "The Widow Lady". **Jim** and **Carmel McHale**, Rooskey, Doocastle, for their help with the story "The Fiddle Player".

Pat Duffy, for his computer work

My wife **Bridie** and son **Joseph** for their patience and support.

My customers and session musicians for their inspiration.

Dedications

THIS BOOK IS DEDICATED to the following people—my mother in law Bridget Grogan RIP, my brother in law, box player Dermot Grogan – RIP, and to my parents RIP.

To a special lady, who gave me grinds in Maths and English, Mrs. Linda Birmingham – RIP.

CHAPTER 1

The Guitar Kid

IT'S A SUNDAY MORNING, not a nice morning for John, he looks up at the ceiling – thinking, thinking.

He heard it all last night, his father and mother shouting at each other, this time last year his mother pulled out because his father gave her a black eye. In the estate where John lives the neighbours are always quarrelling.

His Mother came back in a few days to look after the family, some family John thinks, looking at the ceiling. Mary, in the next room has a six months old baby boy – no husband.

His other sister Margaret who lives next door, has two boys, she and her husband have split up a few years earlier.

Some set up, he thinks to himself, but he is trying to be positive.

He turns on the heavy metal music; he looks over at his guitar in the corner and wonders will he ever make it or is it just a dream.

Noel and Liam Gallagher made it, he thinks, and they lived in a Council estate in Manchester, so why couldn't he?

He loves Bob Geldof – "Rat Trap" is his favourite track.

Someday, someday, he dreams, he will get the break.

"Come down John, your breakfast is ready" his Mother shouts, "you have to go to Mass".

Bridget is his Mother's name, a very religious woman; her family has no time for her since she married his father. "A bum and an alcoholic" they called him.

Her brothers, both priests, don't come near the place.

His father could never hold down a job, a fancy boy in the pub and bookie office, and could be very nasty in the house.

It was his mother's sister in America who kept the family going, sending money and clothes.

His father couldn't hold money; it would be spent in the bookies or the pub.

One night he heard his mother crying to her sister on the phone, when his Father did not come home.

John picks up his guitar and puts it in the cupboard under lock and key. After Mass he will play it again. It's not too fancy, he bought it for a fiver at an auction. Thanks to Malachy his friend down the road, twenty pounds put new strings and a coat of varnish on it. He hopes to buy a better one when he starts working.

John sits down at the table, afraid to look up at this mother's face, as he knows she has been crying. He knows she has Masses read for his father to stop drinking, but it's no good. She even lights candles for him after Mass.

John and his mother are very close; when he was younger she would sit up till late telling him stories about her own father who played in a band, and also, her mother who left her and her family when they were very young.

Sometimes when he came home from school, he would find his mother on her own in his room crying, looking at her wedding photographs. Drying her eyes she would say "John, play something for me on the guitar".

When he would strum the guitar playing "Johnny be Good" her eyes would light up, smiling she would say "You'll make it John, I know you'll it make John".

John's dreaming is disturbed by his mother's voice telling him its time for Mass.

"We'll walk down by the back of the house" she says, "We don't want the neighbours staring at us".

John stands up and holds his mother's hand, "Plenty of time Mum, we have plenty of time".

He looks small for his age, he's just thirteen, but when his mother looks at him and sees the sunshine in his eyes and his clean blonde hair, it helps her forget, for the time being, about the situation she is living in.

John and his mother enter the church. The sound of the choir brings a smile to his face. He loves to hear the choir and the guitar in the background, he blesses himself and looks up at the choir thinking about a song he heard with the same rhythm.

His mother looks pious with John beside her as she walks up to the front seats.

She likes to look at "Our Lord" on the cross with St Joseph and Our Lady on either side.

John is still trying to remember where he heard that song before with the same choir music.

The priest walks on to the altar but John is not paying too much attention to him, he doesn't like priests.

He feels they don't really help people, all they do is tell them how they should live.

They didn't give much help to his mother when she needed it.

Big deal he thinks, looking up at his fancy costume.

Where did he hear that choir music? – "Yes" he says, out loud, disturbing his patrons beside him in the seat, it was Michael Jackson in the RDS.

He watched the concert on television a few years earlier.

His Mother looks down at him, putting her finger to her mouth saying "shush"

Looking at her, John smiles and thinks she should have been a nun.

John looks at the cross with the crown of thorns and says a short prayer

"God if you're out there, help me Mam, and if you have any time to spare, help me to play the guitar and make a few pounds, thank you God".

Watching his mother walking up the aisle to receive at the altar, he notices all the pious people, some young some old and he wonders what is this religion all about, but if it helps his mother what does it matter.

They stand up together at the end of the Mass and when he looks up at the balcony, he sees Malachy who was playing the guitar. He waves to him, Malachy waves back and smiles.

They play together sometimes at Malachy's place and by God, John thinks, he's good.

Leaving the church with his mother, it starts to rain, good he thinks, it will be a good excuse to go to his room and practice.

Who knows what the future holds for the guitar kid?

CHAPTER 2

The Ball Alley

"It's time John" Mary says looking at her watch.

"We will be late for the flight".

"All right Mary I just want to look at the old sod before we go".

John and Mary had been home on holidays from New York for a week and had stayed in Ballina in a guest house.

John was born in Knockmore and had not been home for thirty years.

The place is closed up now. The roof fallen in and the windows all cracked.

Mary, John's wife is a yank of Irish parents, it's her first time in Ireland and she hates every minute of it.

John has spent the last hour looking around the old house, doesn't go inside, it doesn't hold too many fond memories for him, his father was a drunkard and not too good to his wife, two sisters, one retarded, died in an institution, the other married in Chicago to a cop.

Standing outside the small window, he remembers one night his father came home drunk, from Ballina, shouting at his mother, he often lay in the bed in a cold sweat.

His father got drowned one night in a drain on his way home from the pub,

John was only ten years old at the time. He never returned to visit the grave after the funereal, even though his father's sister begged him to go.

He said "no", he was a bad man, I don't want to think of him anymore. Even after fifty years he still does not want to go to the graveyard.

"Come on" Mary says "Its time we were going, it's a long journey to Shannon"

Her voice bounces John back to reality "All right Mary we'll go, I don't think I'll be coming back here again"

"No harm" she replies "this place gives me the creeps".

John steers the golf diesel towards the crossroads and just at the back of the sign he sees the remnants of his past, a place he enjoyed in his youth with his friends, a place to escape from reality, the old ball alley. John stops the car again.

"Whats wrong "? asks his wife "hurry up and drive on, we have a long journey ahead, or else I'll ring a taxi".

John doesn't hear her, opening the door he dries the tears from his eyes as he moves towards the stone castle, this was his home every Saturday and Sunday, where he enjoyed his handball, playing with the half solid, with Michael Wempsey and Joe Sweeney, and the craic they had afterwards.

John walks across the long grass towards the fading walls, a sign that no one uses it anymore, creeping ivy sticks to the outside, and in the square, weeds growing up through the concrete.

But still the ball alley stands out in honour and defies the take-over of nature, it has stood the test of time, its forty years since John played here.

Standing in the middle of the floor, he bows his head and cries, this was it, every Sunday at two o clock, the half solid the craic with the boys, at least twenty of them, standing around waiting their turn, in hail, rain or snow.

John goes over to the right hand side and pictures himself there years ago. The writing on the wall is gone; nothing showing only large bunches of ivy.

"Hello there, are you lost" a voice comes from behind, looking around he sees the small features of an old man.

"No" he replies "just reminiscing about my youth", he looks squarely at the old man, shading his eyes from the sun, he thinks he knows him.

"It's not yourself Paddy?" he asks

"It is surely" the man replies, who might you be he enquires

John Sweeney, he replies

"Handball John" Paddy says,"how are you John, it must be forty years since you were home"?

"It is Paddy" John replies "and how are you?"

"Not too bad John"

"Jesus, man, you're a sight for sore eyes"

The two men shake hands in the middle of the concrete castle, both blending in well with the stature of the place. They stand smiling at each other, "we'll play no more handball here" Paddy says, "well not in this world" John replies.

"Where do you live now Paddy"? He asks,

"In Ballina, in a nursing home, my nephew drops me out here once a week, the house down the road is still there and this time of year I like to stroll around the place".

"Where are you living now" Paddy asks, "In the States" he replies, I've been there now for forty years, I'm just back on holiday, we're going out from Shannon this evening, we had some good days here Paddy"

"We had, John, surely" Paddy replies, "none of the young bucks play here anymore"

"No they don't" John says, surveying the walls, "everything has changed".

"We had some happy days here, John, happy and simple"

"They will probably knock it down shortly" John says "Otherwise someone might get hurt"

"They won't John, it holds the last bit of history around the place, and it is an attraction for tourists"

John dries the tears from his eyes, and thinks this will be his last trip; he won't see the ball alley again.

"You haven't got a camera, Paddy, have you?" John asks

"No, I haven't" he replies, "but here, take this, I found it in the house a year ago"

Paddy puts his hand in his pocket and hands John a small round ball, a half solid.

"Thanks" John says "it will go to the grave with me"

John bounces the ball ever so slowly on the ground and says "If I was only a bit younger Paddy, we could have a game"

"Not anymore John" Paddy replies "we've had our day"

"I will have to move Paddy, the quare one is waiting in the car, and these Yankee women, I'm sorry to say have no patience.

John holds out his hand to his friend and says" maybe in the next world, they might have one of these places, Paddy.

"You'd never know" Paddy says, laughing "I don't think St Peter would stop us playing

John walks out of the ball alley on to the long grass, looking back at his friend, he holds the half solid in his hand and waves goodbye.

Paddy responds with a smile and a wave.

Moving towards the car, John sees a taxi pulling away with Mary, towards the Galway road.

"God help us, Mary: but you're in an awful hurry, but you'll still have to wait for me in Shannon, because I have the tickets"

John starts his car and moves slowly out to the main road, looking at the concrete walls, he notices the ivy is blowing ever so slightly as if saying goodbye to him.

He takes out the half solid and holds it in his left hand for a minute, before putting it back in his pocket.

"When I go, you will go with me" he says, and you never know St Peter and myself might have a game yet, or maybe the devil" he laughs.

Putting his foot down, John moves up the Galway road towards Shannon, behind him the ivy has stopped blowing on his childhood dream – the ballalley

CHAPTER 3

The Football Match

It's a wet Sunday in June, not a great day for a football match, then again, what day is?

This day has been talked about in Clifden for the last month, itemised in the pubs, football players form checked and double checked, everybody coming to the conclusion that the small team of Clifden is no good, why? – because they have never won anything in the last ten years, and today should be no different.

Clifden plays Tuam in the first round; at home, today in the Odlum's cup and nobody gives the home side much chance.

The trainer is from Dublin, John Fitzgerald, a man who has given his life to football, as a matter of fact his son John junior is goalkeeper, much to the dislike of the captain Michael O'Malley, but then the trainer and captain never got on that well, at several training sessions it nearly came to blows between the two of them.

John, is very strict on training and Michael not agreeing with his tactics.

Its eleven o clock, the match doesn't start until three, John walks around the pitch, thinking about all the talk he heard in the last month, about himself and the group of lads he trains.

The Sunday newspaper this morning reads "No Chance for Clifden, Tuam boys hold the key to success". Bullshit thinks John, my team of lads are as good as you'll get, he thinks, and today I will prove those media cowboys wrong.

He wonders what he will do about Michael, a brilliant footballer, but too self willed. The team voted him captain even though he hardly ever turned up for training sessions, and he seemed to be always in trouble, on, or off the field.

His thinking is disturbed by the sound of two young lads with Clifden jerseys, not far away from him, "will we win today?" they shout at John, with a smile and excitement in their eyes.

"We will" John replies, "we will win, you can be sure".

The two young lads run up the field shouting "Up Clifden, Up Clifden".

John smiles, looking after them, "with the help of God" he says, blessing himself.

"Are you up yet Michael" Mary shouts "its Sunday, time to spend some time in Church",

Michael is wide awake, has been for the last two hours, had a few drinks last night with the team. Not too many, he has to show a little bit of leadership. What's the point he thinks, we're not going to win. Five of the Galway team are playing with Tuam, what chance have we? He thinks. This bloody Dublin trainer, we never got on, his attitude was all wrong, time, time, always on time for training, they would work you into the ground, wet or dry.

Michael doesn't like the son either, he took a lady off him in the disco a year earlier, a real beauty, Mary, fancy talker, big car.

Michael is a block layer, living with his mother and sister, Eileen.

Eileen is in a wheelchair, since a road accident, in which their father Pat was killed.

His father played football for the Clifden club for years, Michael looked up to his father, and his name was held in very high esteem in the area. The stand in the football pitch was named after him "The Pat O'Malley stand"

Michael loves football and he has plenty of medals to prove it, since his Dad died, working on a building site, looking after his Mother and sister, the training sessions have become rather strenuous. Sometimes he feels like packing it all in, yet he has certain qualities which the team admires, leadership, good scoring power, good physique, all the things give him the respect of his teammates, on and off the field.

"I will be down in ten minutes," he shouts "a fast cup of tea and I will hit for Mass".

He looks in the bathroom mirror and says to himself: Michael, hold the head today and don't hit anyone".

As John walks towards the church, he notices there are no flags out on the houses, you wouldn't think there was a match on at all, just upon entering the chuch John sees the captain , Michael, in the distance coming in a different gate. There is a moments stare between the two of them.

"A wet sort of a day" John says to the captain.

"Never noticed" Michael replies in an angry voice.

"I shouldn't have asked" John says.

The two men enter the church, with a giggle from some of the crowd at the doorway. Every one in Clifden knows that the trainer and the captain don't agree.

During the Mass, the priest makes a short phrase saying he wishes the Cliften team all the best on the day, he compliments the trainer and team on their hard work.

Michael smiles over at John in the far seat, giving him the thumbs up for victory.

John returns the smile, with the thumbs up also. Michael knows it is a big match and will compromise with the trainer.

The mass ends and everybody leaves except Michael and John, as if they they know what each other are thinking.

The team are assembled at the back of the church , wondering what is wrong, are they going to have an argument. They were supposed to have a meeting with John before the match. They stare down at the two men sitting motionless in their seats. John is the first to move, then Michael, the two of them meeting each other in the centre aisle.

"Why we don't get on? " Michael says "I don't know maybe it's my fault, maybe it's yours, but I'm willing to compromise for today – Mr Dublin man."

"I give you my hand in friendship, and my team and myself will give it our very best shot"

John holds out his hand and says "thank you sir, this game means a lot to me, you're a good captain and a leader of men.

Moving slowly out of the church, the team shakes hands with the trainer and captain, each man with a determination that he will do his best for his mates, and the two men they admire. There is not much excitement outside the church.

The tricolour blows briskly, with the two club flags on either side, there is a large contingent of Tuam supporters in the stand, noticeable by their colours of yellow and white.

On the other side, there is only a small crowd of Clifden supporters, their flags not noticeable, with the opposing team supporters outnumbering them at about ten to one.

The local band play a Galway tune as they march around the field, their green uniforms shining in the summer sun.

Michael leads his team in the front gate, John watches them from the dressing room, looking at their physique, he thinks they don't look too bad.

Michael goes over to him and asks him for a favour.

"What is it?" John asks.

"Can you send someone to collect my mother and sister Eileen, she is confined to a wheelchair, I would appreciate it" Michael says.

"I will not, I will collect them myself" John replies "the exercise will do me good, your sister and mother will sit with me in the trainers section."

"Thank you" Michael says, holding out his hand.

News travels fast in a small area, the local GAA supporters said that John & Michael had made friends or the match. The locals in the pub laughed when they heard the news.

No way he said those two could never get on, they couldn't drink in the same pub without arguing.

John walks down the town feeling the eyes of the people on him, "where is he going"? Jack asks the woman in the paper shop, "he should be on the pitch, and the match starts in an hour".

A large crowd of drinkers stand outside Paddy Mac's pub, watching him walk down the town.

John takes a right turn to Mountain View estate and knocks at number twenty.

Michael's mother appears at the door wondering what is wrong.

"Michael is not here "she says, "did you and him have a row?" she asks

"I know where your son is" John replies, "he sent me on an errand to collect you and your daughter Eileen"

"He must be going crazy, we have not been at a football match since my husband died" she says, blessing herself.

"Well you are going to this one, by hook or by crook, it's his request, not mine"

"Eileen will catch cold" Mary says "

"She won't" he replies "she will be along with me in the trainers section, well have a flask of tea" between us

Eileen in the background hears the talk and says "I never saw Michael playing and you know how much I love football"

Mary goes down on her knees, crying, "I know you do" tears forming in their eyes as they hold each other.

Mary goes back into the kitchen for Eileen's coat and scarf; she looks up at her husbands photograph over the range. Going out to the sitting room she takes out his scarf and puts it around her neck, saying "your Father wore this to all the matches, he will be with us in spirit today Eileen" she says.

John moves the wheelchair out the gate; there is a smile on Eileen's face as she rubs the scarf with her hand. Mary follows behind them, trying to stop the tears with her hankie.

As the three of them move out of the estate towards the football ground, there is a slight flutter of excitement. People watching from pubs, cars stopping, the town stares at Mary and the trainer pushing the wheelchair towards the gate.

"That's her husband's scarf, Mary is wearing" Michael says to his mate outside Paddy Mac's pub, "he wore it to all the football matches before he died".

The customers stare out of the pub as the three pass by.

"Sorry lads" Paddy Mac says " myself and that girl's father went to all the matches together, Lord rest his soul, the bar is closed until the match is over, if Clifden win, there will be a free bar".

The boys leave the pub, they notice the town is coming to life, shops are closed, and people are parking their cars and moving towards the pitch.

As the publican pulls the door behind him, all his customers follow him towards the pitch, maybe there is hope for this town yet, they think.

As John wheels Eileen, he notices that Mary is smiling at her daughter; also there are a lot of smiles as they move towards the big game. A large crowd of people follow behind them.

News travels fast in a small town, especially when a famous footballer's wife is going to a match with an enemy of her son. Eileen smiles as she looks up at her mother.

Entering the playing area, Eileen is wheeled towards the dug out.

"If you are cold here, say so, this is the best place to view the match" John says

The Clifden stand fills up slowly, one hour earlier there were only a few children in it, now there are five hundred or more, none of them were bothered until they saw what was happening, a rare occasion and a great one for the town.

They cast their eye on the stand, named after Michael's father, and they think of years ago when he entertained them, and won two all Ireland club titles.

As the crowd swells the colour starts to change, the Clifden flags seem to shine a little brighter in the sun, and there is an increase in the euphoria over the whole field.

The two teams are in their dressing room with twenty minutes to go, the Tuam team are not too bothered about the opposition, they are treating it as a practice match until they meet Corofin in the final. Why should they be bothered, five of their team have all Ireland medals. They joke among themselves about having a few pints in Biddy Riley's in Tuam after the match.

The Clifden team walk up and down the dressing room, testing their boots, turning their necks along with other exercises. Michael sits in the corner, waiting for the trainer to appear. John walks in wearing a black track suit and runners; he has a stare in his eyes.

"Michael" he says "your sister and mother are here, your sister will have to go behind the mesh, as some of the committee say its too cold in the dugout, not my decision"

"I know that" Michael says "maybe I should not have brought them here at all"

"Don't talk daft" John says, "she is wearing your father's scarf, she is very proud of you, she will be watching the game like a hawk, win or lose she is going to enjoy the day"

John asks the team to stand up, "Lads" he says "you are a football team, all of you, good if not better than anything in the county; we are playing a good team, strong and confident, but still only a team. I have trained you, I have shouted at you and I have told you things you might not have liked to hear, out there on the field is where it all matters. He points to number twelve Dempsey, "you are centrefield, you can make the difference, you grab the ball and kick" Dempsey nods in agreement.

"No messing, just a good clean game, I will finish on this point, we are playing on our own ground and we will win today, despite all the bullshit talk in the media" says John.

"Good luck lads, we'll talk at half time, and Michael, I don't want your sweat today, I want your blood"

Michael smiles back at him "I don't think I have any"

John and Michael shake hands, the captain looking back at his team saying "come on lads, we have a battle to win"

The band strikes up the "Galway Shawl", they are a local band from the area, and they suit the day and the atmosphere.

The two teams march on to the field, one from the left and the other from the right passing the ball between them. The Tuam team looks smart, the jerseys shining against the sun, their players full of confidence, there should be no trouble with this opposition they think.

The shouts from the Tuam stand are loud, but there is something different today.

The Clifden colours decorate the far side of the field blocking out the sun, the stand that was empty a while ago, is now full of colour, flags caps and buntings. They have come to see their team play, and to see how the captain and trainer plan to win the match.

Michael and his team run up and down the field, passing the ball around, they are not disturbed by the sound of the crowd, they have come here to win. They have belief in themselves, this started in the church with John and Michael shaking hands, the two never got on, and probably never will, but today its friendship, the team, the trainer and the captain. What happens when the game is over, no one knows, or what tomorrow will bring?

Michael goes over to the trainers bunk and enquires where is his sister

John says "she is over there behind the wire at the entrance"

Michael runs over to her with a tear in his eye, and as the gate opens he goes to his mother and holds her, then he kneels down to kiss his sister. Rubbing the scarf around her neck he says, "Dad is with us today and we will win"

He marches back on to the field, rubbing the tears from his eyes. The band strike up playing a marching tune. Michael leads his team in a straight line, he smiles over at the opposing captain, he knows him well, Seamus Quinn, an accountant in Galway, a cocky little boy who fancies himself. I will take that smile off his face before the day is out Michael thinks.

The teams take up their positions, Michael moves to centre field, and he takes a quick glance up at his father's name on the stand and blesses himself. The bandsman signals for the national anthem and everybody stands showing respect for their county. There is no major excitement in any of the stands, Tuam supporters fully confident of success, and the Clifden supporters still wondering about the trainer and captain.

The young lads at the front of the stand wave their flags shouting "come on Clifden, Michael you're a star" they know him from the housing estate, and he has shown them how to play football. Michael has refereed many matches for them. A lot of the kids are from broken homes, and with no dad around the house, Michael is a sort of a father figure.

The ball is thrown in and the game begins, Clifden playing with the wind, Michael catches the ball from the throw in and sends it along the left hand side, one of his team mates is too slow and the Tuam man gets it and sends it down the field, the full forward gets it and sends it over the bar, Tuam get the first point.

Clifden are controlling the game at centre field, but just cannot score. The Tuam team are faster and stronger, twenty minutes into the first half, Tuam are five points to no score from Clifden.

John looks out from the sideline, walking up and down; he decides to replace Brady with Shanagher, who is taller and stronger. Michael agrees with the change. Passing the ball to his mate Sheerin passes it to Grady, Grady gives it to Shannagher, passing it back to Grady again, who buries it in the net.

The Clifden stand comes alive with excitement, the shouts and roars bring an immediate upsurge of confidence to the Clifden team. Mary in the wheelchair waves her scarf, while her mother holds the cross, around her neck. Johnny Mac looks down at the mother and daughter in front of him and thinks about Michael's father in the days gone by.

If Clifden win today, he thinks, it will be a day to remember, and there will be a fair drink in the pub tonight.

The Tuam team move the ball up the field, their confidence not rocked by the Clifden goal; the captain plays the ball to his mate, Dempsey, a big rugged fellow, fourteen stone.

Dempsey gets through the back line and tries for a goal. John junior dives and saves the ball, and clears it to centre field, he hears his father shout "well saved"

Michael catches the ball and passes to Smith, who is pushed in the back and is awarded a free. Michael takes the free and sends it over the bar. The scoreboard reads Clifden, one goal and one point, Tuam five points.

The referee blows for half time.

Michael and his team enter the dressing room, tired and sweating, though not disappointed. They still have a chance to win. The drinks are passed around, bottles of lucozade, ballygowan. They are not talking, they expect John to walk in at any time, and they smile at Michael, with his hands around his head. Michael thinks when the jackeen arrives, there will be trouble, there usually is at half time.

John walks in to the dressing room and looks around saying "how are you feeling lads, no injuries, no pains"?

Nobody answers, they just nod their heads.

"You are doing well lads, the Tuam team are playing well, but we have knocked them a bit, they are not showing any signs of fatigue. The next half we will have to use different tactics.

"Michael, you are slipping a bit, you are not getting the ball quickly enough, and when you do get it , you are not passing it Shanagher quickly enough".

Michael looks up at the trainer and thinks he is some cowboy, "how can I pass it, with two Tuam men looking up my arse every time I turn" he shouts at the trainer.

"I know they are watching you" John shouts back "you'll have to move faster, otherwise you'll get hurt Michael, those two boys that are marking you are tough, and they got two yellow cards at their last game".

"Give me McNeill, instead of Sheerin, he's taller and faster" Michael shouts.

"All right" John shouts "I'll give you McNeill, but kick that fucking ball, when you get it, if you get hurt the game is lost, and they will try anything the second half".

John looks over at his son and says "good save, be careful of that Sweeney fella, don't tackle him, right lads, I have no more to say, we can win this game with plenty of sweat, we might get burned, but we will win".

Michael stirs himself from the corner, shouting, "right lads, it's time to move, is everybody all right"? He asks.

There is a mixture of comments, but the game will be played, win or lose, and the team know they have a leader in their captain.

The Clifden team get a loud cheer when they come out on the field, Michael looks over towards his mother and sister, and waves to them.

Eillenn waves back to him, win or lose Michael thinks, it's the first time he has seen her smile for years.

The Tuam team look a bit tired, their jerseys are not quite as clean as when the game started, sill, their confidence is not broken. They have played a few games like this before, and they have won.

Michael hits for centre field, looking over at John, he thinks, "you are so dramatic, ice cold features.

Michael knows a win would put a feather in John's cap, rumour has it that the board were going to replace him, if he didn't show results before the end of the season.

John has trained some good teams in the past with good results, but the the Clifden Team didn't answer to the call, his third year in the job, and no great results so far.

Last years game was a disaster, everybody in Clifden laughing after the performance; it was the talk of the place for months. John the trainer, taking the blame .

Michael getting the stick at training sessions, it nearly came to blows a few times in the dressing room.

The referee throws in the ball; Michael grabs it and kicks it down the field. Clifden are playing into the wind, the ball is picked up by Jimmy O'Dea, the Clifden full forward, he kicks it over the bar.

A good start John thinks, the sides are level, if only Michael can hold the head, we have a good chance, "I'm always giving out to him, to hold the head, either he is injured, or sent off for fouling.

John walks up and down, watching the other trainers from across the field. James Owens, a Tipperary man, a good trainer, it's his first year with the team.

This is my third year, John reminds himself.

The Tuam trainer makes a fast substitution. The game continues, heavy tackling, three yellow cards, two for Tuam, one for Clifden. The two sides are locked in battle. Tuam get a point from a free, Clifden convert a fifty.

The sides are level for the second time; the crowd are beginning to believe in the home side, shouts coming with an air of confidence from Clifden stand.

Paddy Mac shouts "come on Michael, it is your day", thinking if only Michael's father were here, maybe he is, he thinks.

Michael catches a long ball and goes to pass it to his team mate O'Dwyer, as he is about to fist it, two Tuam men tackle him, knocking him to the ground. O'Dwyer rushes in to help, the three men collide, Michael gets caught with Dwyer's boot by accident.

Michael goes down, unconscious. He comes around to the sound of the crowd shouting, trying to get up; he falls down again, blacking out. He sees a cloud before his eyes and hears a voice.

"Who is that"? Michael mutters.

"It's your father" the voice replies.

"Is that you Da"? enquires Michael

"I'm watching you today, you are playing well, but you must score a goal to win the game, kick the ball to McNeill then rush in to the goalmouth for the return pass and take your goal. God bless you son" the voice says.

Michael mutters "goodbye Da"

Michael wakes to the sound of the crowd, a doctor looking down on him "are you all right Michael"? he asks, "you were unconscious and muttering something about your Da"

The doctor says "if you want Michael we will take you off"

"No" he replies, "how much time is left?"

"Two minutes to go" the trainer replies.

Michael rises to his feet, dizzy, but ready to go. He waves over to his sister and mother and tells the trainer to go and tell them he is all right.

The referee holds Michael by the arm and tells him to hurry up saying one minute to go plus injury time.

Michael sets the ball for the free kick, thinking about his dream; he picks out McNeill to the left of the goalmouth. Kicking the ball he moves like lighting towards the Tuam goals.

McNeill jumps for the ball and misses it, he quickly retrieves it from the Tuam man.

Michael shouts for the ball, McNeill kicks it towards the Tuam goals, Michael jumps for it, seeing an opening in the Tuam defence, he moves to his left and kicks, the Tuam goalkeeper, sees it coming, but too late, missing the ball by inches.

The people on the Clifden stand cannot believe their eyes, where did Michael come from?.

The Tuam supporters stare at the ground, puzzled by what has happened, the shouts of the home supporters echo around the field.

Tears flow from Paddy Mac's eyes, clapping, he thinks, what is in the cat is in the puisin, just like his father.

John walks up the field, clapping and shouting to the supporters behind him.

"We've won lads, we've won!

The referee blows the final whistle and the pitch comes alive with excitement.

Michael sits down, hands over his head. Looking up at his father's stand, he thinks, coincidence maybe, maybe not, it doesn't matter, we've won.

The trainer walks over and holds out his hand to lift him up, the two men hold one another in an embrace, while the supporters clap them on their backs.

"Come on" says John, it's time to make a speech.

"You must be joking" Michael replies.

"I am not joking; the team and the supporters expect it, just a few words"

Michael walks over to the stand, amid claps on the back, walking up the steps, he waves to his mother and sister.

John holds the microphone and asks for ciunas., "Michael wants to say a few words" he says.

Michael takes the microphone and begins "I would like to thank the Tuam team for a great game, give the Tuam team a big clap" he says to the several hundred people in front of him.

"We have not won this cup today, we played football not for a cup, but for the love of the game. I would like to thank my team mates for training so hard, our trainer who gave us his time and devotion. Lastly, our supporters who gave us belief in ourselves and in our colours.

His team mates hold him shoulder high, shouting "Up Clifden" carrying him down the field.

John watches them from the sideline, we will have to train harder for the next game, he thinks.

He looks over at Michael's mother and sister, his mother pushing the wheelchair, the crowd moving aside to let them through.

"Great game "Paddy Mac says to her, "a great lad, that son of yours, your husband would be a proud man today.

Mary smiles and says "thank you Paddy, you and him were good friends.

The football ground is nearly empty now, except for a few birds picking around the muddy goalmouths.

There was no rain during the match and the sun is now setting slowly.

John walks around the field, reflecting on the day. He wonders what he will do with Michael, he worries that he will go on the beer. "We will worry about that next Thursday when the training starts.

Walking out the side gate, he hears music coming from Mac's pub. The supporters are happy. Michael is there with a pint, he won't be singing, but he will be the star attraction.

A free bar and plenty of talk about his fantastic goal.

Mary is back at home, Eileen is in the sitting room watching television. Mary looks up at her husbands photograph over the range and smiles "you were there today love, you were there" she says to herself.

She hopes that Michael won't be too late as he has to go to work on Monday.

There is a Mass for his father Tuesday. It was this day five years earlier he died, it was at four o clock she heard the dreadful news.

CHAPTER 4

The Hound of Cuchulainn

MICHAEL IS OLD NOW, he lives on his own.

Mary died 4 years ago this Christmas, they have no family and both are very much attached to one another.

Michael looked after her for two years before she died, his life is not much different to anyone else's here, four days before Christmas.

He smokes his pipe, looking at the open fire; he is not concerned too much about the troubles of the world.

Sitting beside Michael is his best mate Butch, a hound who is his only friend.

They look at one another, Michael smiles down at him and the large dog bows his head in friendship.

The kitchen is not too well decorated, bits of holly over the fireplace, nothing too fancy.

Michael does not go to town now, he's too old, but he is a hunting man, and every day Butch and himself would walk around the old farm, Butch too old to run after rabbits and Michael happy now to look at nature and enjoy its beauty.

Michael looks over the fireplace at the photos, some of them are forty years old, his wife Mary and himself on their wedding day, and another taken ten years earlier with his dog Butch.

Himself and Mary with the cup in the middle, showing his dog at a show in Killybegs, they nicknamed his dog "The Hound of Cuchulainn".

"We're getting old Butch" he says, looking down at his mate, he thinks of ten years ago "surely you were a beauty then, people called to the house to see you, and take photographs, they said you're breeding was top class, and that you descended from the hound of Cuchulainn, large handsome and swift".

"Time takes its toll on us all" he says, "I am old but you're still a good looking dog, what will happen when I go Butch, what will you do, I only hope we go together" he says, rubbing the dog's long nose, "when the man calls me up I hope you will be beside me Butch, you, me and Mary, together in that far off land".

The large dog stands up and walks around the kitchen, he may be old but he would still draw an eye from anyone who knows about dogs, tall, solid features, handsome face, and the breeding top class. When they named him after Cuchulainns dog they were not too far wrong.

Butch was well known in the area, and had his name in the paper several times, mostly for dog shows, but his biggest prize came six years earlier when he received an award from the Irish president for saving a child's life.

Michael and his dog were walking in the glens one summer's day when he thought he heard a shout from the top of the hill; he thought he might have been dreaming.

There were a lot of sounds around in the middle of summer, crows, cuckoos and other wildlife. Butch started barking and ran up the mountain; Michael couldn't run that fast, so he walked steadily to the top of the hill overlooking a lake.

The far side of the hill was steep, Butch barked louder as Michael noticed two people in the distance, one of them seemed to be limping while the other man was holding on to him. Seemingly they had an accident earlier, both of them were mountaineers.

There were a lot of tourists around this area in the summer, and a lot of French people were hunting or mountaineering.

Michael shouts down from the hill "Are you all right"? The two French tourists nod in approval, speaking in a foreign accent that Michael does not fully understand.

Butch climbs down the hill and makes his way towards the climbers, one of them limping very badly, a young lad about fifteen, the other man is his father, both were lost and the young lad was sweating very badly.

Butch approaches the lad and licks his hands while his father shows signs of fear, he has been carrying the young lad all night.

The father takes out a long rope and gives it to the dog, Butch runs up the mountain again.

Michael takes the rope and ties around a tree. Father and son try to ascend the hill, but it's no good, the young lad keeps falling down. Eventually the father climbs up the mountain and Butch carries the rope down to the young lad who ties it around himself. Butch climbs up the mountain again. Michael and the Frenchman pull hard on the rope but to no avail.

Eventually Michael ties the rope around the dog's neck, shouting "Come on Butch, pull, pull".

Butch and Michael use all their strength and the young lad moves slowly up the mountain, shouting in pain.

Pulling him in Michael notices the lad is shivering with pain. "Go Butch and get the brandy and bring it here" he commands the dog "In the top of the cabinet".

Michael covers the young lad with his jacket as Butch takes off at a terrific speed towards the house two miles away.

The back door is open; he hopes the dog can get in.

The young lad's father says something that Michael doesn't understand, but he shakes his hand with tears in his eyes.

"Hurry up Butch, this young lad could catch pneumonia".

Butch races of towards Michel's house in the distance, running like a hare, long strides, he knows what Michael wants, and he trained him as a pup to fetch bottles of water when they were in the bog.

Butch knows what he must do, Michael always leaves the back door unlocked, he races up to the house and catches the lock by his teeth to open it, going in to the kitchen, and he knows where Michael keeps the brandy.

That's all Michael drinks, a few pints in the pub, and a brandy for medicinal purposes. When Butch's master suffers from a cold, the dog would have to go to town for a paper, meat, and even a noggin of brandy.

Jim, the owner of the shop and pub would often ring to see if Michael was all right, especially after his wife's death. He would always know what to give the dog when he arrived. Some smart young fellow tried to rob him one day, he was carrying the shopping in a plastic bag, to his dismay he had to get five stitches in hand.

He reported the incident to the gardai, and they said if it happened again the dog would have to be put down.

Michael looks at the young lad who's shaking with the cold, they were climbing the previous day and got lost, they slept in a cave overnight. Michael knows the cave very well, "Bear Cave" it's called, legend has it that bears lived in this cave at one time.

The father and son don't speak much English, but Michael sees many tourists around here, mostly fishermen and he knows how to communicate with them.

Going to the cupboard, Butch climbs up on the cabinet and takes hold of the plastic bag. He knows about the brandy, Michael has been sick many times, he has often brought brandy to him in bed when Mary was in hospital.

Moving through the door Butch holds the plastic bag in his mouth and races towards the hill where his master is waiting.

Michael looks down the mountain wondering what has happened to Butch. Suddenly in the distance he sees the large animal coming towards him. The dog moves in long strides, his beauty showing against the sun, surely you are a handsome dog, Michael thinks.

Michael takes the bag from the dog's mouth, opening the bottle he gives a thimble full to the young lad, who is now shaking badly.

He turns to the boy's father and tells him to remove his rucksack, Michael takes the young lads rucksack and ties them together, explaining to the father he is going to make a stretcher out of them.

He ties the rope to the dog's collar and feeds it through the dog's mouth. "We have to pull this lad to safety, he is not able to walk, try your best Butch, and try your best" he says, rubbing the dogs back.

Butch pulls the sleigh ever so slowly, stopping now and then to get his breath, his long legs showing signs of strain; he continues to pull the young lad towards the house.

As Michael and his crew near the house, he rubs the dog's back saying "you're a brave one Butch, you're a brave one. Opening the kitchen door, they lift the child on to the bed; the boy is nearly unconscious with the pain, shaking with the cold.

Dialing the emergency code, Michaels calls for an ambulance and a doctor. The ambulance takes the child to Letterkenny hospital where he is diagnosed with pneumonia and a broken ankle.

The father of the child holds Michaels hands with tears in his eyes, and goes down on his knees and puts his arms around the tired dog, speechless, he walks out the door wiping the tears with his handkerchief.

Mary returns from hospital a few days later, hearing the news from Michael, she looks over at Butch in the corner, smiling she says "you deserve a medal, you are a brave one".

Michael doesn't say much, looking at his wife, he knows the she has the buck and she has to go to hospital once a month for chemotherapy.

The doctor says she has about eighteen months to two years to live, before the boss man calls her up.

Michael hears a knock on the door, "come in if you're decent, if you're not, stop out" he says.

The postman, Jim Dunleavy opens the door, "you were here this morning already, is there anything wrong"

"No" Jim replies "just sign this and I'll be on my way"

Michael takes the biro and signs his name, "what is it Jim"?

"I don't know he says, but it came from Dublin an hour ago, marked urgent".

Michael opens the letter and looks at it, and then he sits down in shock,"

"By God Mary look at this, it's a letter from the Irish president, that man we helped was the French ambassador to this country, he was traveling incognito in Donegal, he has recommended a medal for Butch and myself, there will be a car here next Thursday to bring us to Dublin".

According to this the hotel will be paid for, and there will be a French band at the ceremony".

News travels fast in a small area, the following Tuesday it made the front page of "The Donegal Democrat"

The headline read "Superdog to get award from president, French ambassador shows respect for hound of Cuchullan".

A state car calls on Thursday at eight o clock; Michael, Mary and Butch are brought to Dublin. Michael enjoys the scenery, its years since he was in Dublin. Butch sits as proud as punch between the two of them.

When they arrive at the Clarence hotel, a porter opens the door for them. Michael and his wife walk in, people stare at the huge animal. Michael is greeted by the hotel manager who tells them there is a room paid for them; the dog will have to eat downstairs.

"I will have to go down with him, he gets savage on his own" says Michael.

Michael and his wife stay upstairs and Butch stays downstairs, chained in a small room.

The following morning the manager calls them for breakfast, while a taxi man waits outside reading the paper.

Butch is collected by his master at eleven o clock.

When they reach the president's house, every thing seems quiet. Michael in his black suit and white shirt and tie, Mary wears her summer dress, the hound himself, well brushed, his coat shining in the morning sun.

They walk up the steps; the door is opened by the butler who shows them in. Michael stops inside the door, looking around the large room he sees two men sitting down, while at each side a small group begins to play a marching tune.

A man wearing a uniform walks up to Michael and bows, asking him, in broken English to follow him.

Michael and Mary walk up the hall with Butch in the middle on a short leash. When they reach the two men, Michael recognises one of them as the man he met on the mountain; the other man is the Irish president.

The Frenchman salutes Michael and shakes his hand. Taking a medal from the president he places it around Butch's neck, rubbing the dog's head, he takes a step back and salutes him. A small troupe plays the French national anthem.

After the ceremony, Michael gets a tour of the president's residence, and a personal invitation to visit the French president in Paris. After tea, and a chat with the president, they are collected and brought back to Donegal in the state car. They were told they would be receiving photographs in a few weeks.

There wasn't much talk about the visit to Dublin, Michael and his wife didn't want too much publicity.

Six months later, Mary passed away; she died peacefully in her sleep. The cancer treatment stopped working.

Michael sits back on his chair in the kitchen, looking up at the photographs, he thinks the picture of the French diplomat and the president is the nicest one, everyone smiling, and Butch with his tongue hanging out, the medal like a fancy tie around his neck.

We were so proud and happy that day, Michael thinks, he looks over at Butch in the corner and calls him over, "I'm going to have a sleep for an hour, when I wake up we'll have something to eat"

Butch looks up at his master and hands him his paw in recognition. Michael closes his eyes and says a short prayer "Thank you God for the good and happy years".

Dropping his hands by his side he goes into a deep sleep, he dreams of Mary years earlier, dancing in the local hall, and then he dreams of Butch and the day they found him outside their door. He was only a small pup at the time. All of a sudden he finds himself walking in the fields with Butch, in front of him is a small fort, legend had it that the fairies lived there. Michael walks up to the fort, Butch ahead of him disappears in the bushes, a large cloud descends down in front of Michael, through the mist he sees a tall man wearing a kilt. Butch is standing beside him.

"Hello Michael" the man says, "I'm sorry, but Butch cannot stay with you any longer, I want him now, he has another life to live in the next world, thank you Michael" the man says.

"Yourself and Mary were good to my dog, I gave him to you years ago, now I must take him back, When you wake up, your dog will be gone. You will meet him again when your Master calls you up, yourself and Mary and Butch will walk these mountains in spirit in a very short time. Goodbye Michael, till we meet again."

Michael is awakened from his sleep by the banging of the door, funny he thinks , I thought I locked it this evening, opening the door he looks up at the sky, the stars are bright and the moon is full, he hears his dog howling in the far off distance. "Goodbye old friend" Michael says "till we meet again, goodbye".

Michael died shortly afterwards, he was waked in the house, some of the photographs were put in the coffin with him, and the dogs lead was put between his hands. He was buried with his wife in the local graveyard.

A few days later, a man visiting the graveyard, thought he saw a large dog standing beside Michael's grave, when he got closer, there was no dog, just some leaves blowing over the fresh soil.

When people visit Donegal in the summertime and go fishing or mountain climbing, they often report seeing a large dog and a man in the far off hills. Who the man is, nobody knows, sometimes, around Christmas time when people walk by Michael's house, they think they hear a noise, like a dog barking or a woman's voice talking.

Some people say its only folklore, others say it's the wind blowing in the trees, or a fox howling, still others say it's the hound of Cuchulain looking for his master.

CHAPTER 5

The Bog

I'T'S A NICE MORNING in June; the sun is shining, there is lots of activity about the bog land. Nature is at its best at six o clock in the morning.

There are no sounds of tractors or turf machines; they are standing there like buildings, no noise or movement. Nature is undisturbed at this time of day.

The stream surrounded by heather looks clear with a ray of sunshine on it. A hen pheasant moves beside it, picking up whatever nature has to offer.

The rabbits stand motionless, enjoying the sound of the cuckoo as the frogs jump into the water to maintain their colour, large reeks of turf standing motionless provide a hiding place for the ants and flies who do not want to see the sun.

Nature – total nature, undisturbed by man or machinery

The fox moves through the heather, fearful of drawing too much attention to himself, hoping to catch a young pheasant. A soaring hawk peers down in total bewilderment with it all.

The fish in the local stream show their faces, watching the flies move above the water. It is not breakfast time yet as there is a fog over the water. The spider's web is damp with the morning dew; it has to dry before he can expect his catch.

The cow's lie in the neighbouring field listening to the sounds of nature, local thrushes hop around beside them, hoping they will move and reveal a few worms or insects. The badger moves back to his home having fulfilled his appetite the night before

An old building looks down on the stream, once inhabited by local people who left at the time of the famine. The windows are barred up with timber, only a small ray of sunshine can peep through the door, the thatch roof is sagging worn down with years of decay, it's only a summer home for the swallows, yet on a sunny morning it blends in well with local nature. A group of young mice peep through the bottom of the door afraid to venture out too far. A hedgehog moves in slowly to rest for the day; the weather is not suitable for his type of lifestyle.

The sheds beside the thatched house look ghostly with the doors broken; an old milk churn sits abandoned beside the door showing signs of time gone by. The crane beside the door is now rusty, the old pots and skillets beside it look old and weather beaten with the march of time.

The heather around the house blows ever so slightly with the breeze; the yellow cowslips smile out onto the landscape, undisturbed by the local activity.

The sound of a donkey braying creates a slight disturbance, the pheasants in the background look up briefly, and he is part of the action taking place at the moment

Suddenly – a noise which catches everyone by surprise, a tractor roars into life.

The hen pheasants run for cover in the rushes, the hawk descends like an airplane to the ground and there are panic stations everywhere.

The cows in the field move their ears to the strange sounds as the thrushes fly off in a terror; the fox disappears into the heather, disturbed from his plan. The scene becomes chaotic.

A man and his dog are moving up the bog road, both unaware of the panic in front of them.

Nature is disturbed for the time being; tomorrow at five o clock it will open itself to another day of tranquility.

CHAPTER 6
The Fairies

JOHN IS PLAYING in the garden, the birds are singing, its warm on a fine day in June. There is a gentle breeze, noticeable by the slight flutter of the trees; the garden is small by modern standards, palms on both sides shade it from the neighbouring houses, a small fountain features in the centre.

Mary spends a lot of time here, sitting reading; she also finds it a break from the outside world when her husband is at work. Her son John does not hear the birds singing or the sound of distant traffic, John who is only seven, was born deaf and dumb.

Mary smiles at her son, such a young handsome boy and wonders what will the future hold for him, a small tear in her eye.

John smiles back at his mother, he cannot talk to her or hear her, but he has friends of his own, not visible by other humans – The Fairies.

They should be coming out shortly, John smiles to himself, they are his only friends, he talks to them and they laugh and enjoy his company.

There is a slight flutter in the trees and John hears a voice "come on Michael, we haven't got all day, remember we promised John we would play the fiddle for him".

Two little elves smile up at John and say "good morning big man, how are you today"? "Fine "John replies with a whisper only understood by the little people.

"What jig would you like to hear today?" asks the elves.

"I don't know" John replies.

"Well you need to decide quickly; the girls will be here shortly for the dance".

John hears a sound coming from the trees and sees about a dozen fairy ladies, dressed in green with dancing shoes on, all flying down towards Michael. They all alight on the ground, flying and tiptoeing along, smiling up at John.

Michael looks at his friend and asks "Thomas, have you got the bodhran with you"?

"I have" he replies, rushing back to the trees for it.

"Right "he says "we have to wait for the Prince and Princess, they promised they would dance for John today, I hope they haven't forgotten.

Mary, reading her book, gazes over at her son in the garden and sees a large nest of butterflies floating around him.

Her son loves nature, every winter he would come out to the garden to feed the birds bread and nuts, and some of them would eat out of his hand.

The two little men argue with one and other, "Are you sure you told the Prince"? Michael shouts.

"Of course I did" Thomas replies.

"Well then, where is he?" Michael asks, walking around in circles, "the ladies will not dance without him".

There is a disturbance in the corner of the hedge and John hears a bugle blowing, "he's coming" John says, holding his bodhran.

"It's about time" Michael shouts "these young ones today are all spoiled, if his father was alive, he would have a different attitude".

The young Prince comes out from the hedge in a carriage drawn by two black and white horses and stops in front of John.

The door of the carriage opens, the Prince holds out his hand to help the Princess down, both of them smile up at John and bow their heads.

The Prince looks over at the two musicians saying "what's the matter, the two of you look as though you were arguing".

"We were your majesty" they replied, "We thought you might have forgotten".

"You should have known we would not disappoint John!" The Prince said impatiently, "the Princess has brought her fiddle so we can start right away".

Mary looks over at John again and notices he is smiling down at two magpies walking beside him; also there are a lot of butterflies about him, flying up and down in rotation.

"I'll finish the last chapter of the book, then I will have to go and get John's dinner ready" she says to herself.

The Prince gives the order to the ladies to line up; the Princess takes her fiddle from the carriage and gets ready for the dance.

The dancers line up, their costumes shining in the summer sun, as John kneels down on his hunkers with a smile of anticipation on his face.

The Princess resins up the bow and starts to tune in with Michaels fiddle.

All twelve of the ladies form a circle around the Prince.

The Prince leads the group, his feet moving to the beat of the bodhran.

The two fiddles play slowly, not drowning out the sound of the drum.

The ladies in their costumes surround the Prince joining hands with each other, and as the bodhran stops, the fiddles take over to the sound of the beat.

The Prince dances with a style of his own, while the ladies dance around him holding hands.

John is dancing and clapping his hands, tears of joy showing in his eyes.

The ladies float into the air smiling at John.

The Prince and Princess ascend into the air and the Princess kisses John on the cheek.

Mary looks down at John again and sees him clapping his hands, as the butterflies move about him, such innocence she thinks with a smile on her face, nature really loves you John

The music stops abruptly and the dancers bow before John.

Michael shouts up" how did you enjoy that, big man"?

"Wonderful" John replies.

The Prince says "we must go now John, it will be dark shortly and your mother wants to get your dinner, but we'll meet again shortly.

The two elves shout up at John "we will see you tonight before you go to sleep and we will read you a story of the fairies of Nottingham".

Mary taps John on the shoulder and indicates that it's dinner time.

John responds "ok Mammy" using sign language.

As John moves away from the garden towards the door of the house, he stops briefly and waves goodbye to his friends.

They wave back to him saying John "we love you and we always will".

Mary looks down at John and then glances at the butterflies who seem to be John s best friends. Sometimes at night time she finds two or three of them in his room and wonders how they came in.

When she sees the smile on Johns face, his book open beside him, what she can do except open the window and let them out.

CHAPTER 7

Christmas Story

IT'S NOT MUCH OF a Christmas for Sean, living on the side of the road, even though the caravan is well decorated, a car battery outside working the Christmas lights.

Sean's father, has come home drunk, and is now stretched on the couch sleeping.

"Thank God he's settled down at last, in town all day drinking" Sean mutters to himself.

Sean's Mother is with his younger sisters and brothers in the other caravan parked close beside them.

When they wake up they won't have a lot either, even though their mother has bought the turkey and St Vincent de Paul has given them bags full of toys.

Sean looks over at the crib in the corner and thinks about God and the baby born on Christmas Eve and thinks, maybe all travelers are like that – no fixed abode, but still its nice to see the baby infant shining in the corner, with the sheep and cows around him, it gives Sean a warm feeling and brings a small tear to his eye.

He looks up at the cross over the crib and says a little prayer " Help us God on this Christmas Eve, help me Ma and Da, even though we are only traveling people – God, you were a traveler yourself one time and you understand – help Mary, John and Michael and all our family and cousins to have a happy Christmas, and God, don't let Da get drunk, because he might get into trouble" , kissing the cross he wears around his neck, he says "Thank you God".

He lies down to sleep in a corner, pulling his blanket tightly round him, peering out at the cold night. His dreams are filled with fairies and horses. Sean was always a dreamer, he loves music and singing, he remembers Christmases long gone when his mother used to sing him to sleep. The night is colder now; he rubs the glass to look at the snowflakes falling.

"Sean are you there, Sean are you there"! Sean awakes from his sleep to the noise of someone knocking on the caravan window; through the glass he sees it's his Uncle Mick, back from England. Sean covers himself with the blanket and puts on his shoes, opening out the door he sees his uncle sitting in a pony and trap smoking his pipe. "What's wrong Uncle Mick" Sean asks, "Strange to see you on such a night, will I wake Da"? "No no, don't, I'm only passing through". Mick holds out his hand and asks Sean to hold it, when Sean holds it, its as if its cold, not a normal cold but a dead cold, "Sean" he says " you're a good boy, full of life and promise, the life of a traveler is not an easy one Sean, but you're more than a traveler, you descended from a great people, an Irish race that ruled this country years ago – the Celts. A friend of mine will bring you a present in a few days time, take it Sean, it's the pipes of the Celts, they belonged to our people for hundreds of years, you will play them, and God will show you. I'll be off now, – Happy Christmas". "Happy Christmas Uncle Mick" shouts Sean as the wheel tracks fade into the snow.

Sean retreats into the caravan, looking at the clock, its ten past four, he blesses himself and goes back to sleep.

Sean wakes to the sound of a donkey braying, his father is moving himself along the floor of the caravan "Wake up Sean" he says "We have to go to Mass today to say a few prayers for the living and the dead".

Sitting up, Sean replies "I had a dream last night Da, about Uncle Mick".

"You're always dreaming" says his father

"I dreamt he was outside the caravan in a pony and trap, smoking his pipe". Sean's father laughs as he tries to light the gas ring under the kettle.

Sean continues "He told me I would be getting a present in a few days", "what sort of a present"? Asks his father

"A set of uillean pipes, he called them the pipes of the Celts".

His fathers smile changes to a frown and he looks at his son with a stare in his eyes "You must have been dreaming – those pipes are across the water for years, your uncle Mick got them from his father fifty years ago on Christmas Eve, the night his father died"

Sean's father blesses himself "Lord rest his soul"

A garda car pulls in , silently, in the snow and two garda get out. Sean opens the door and sees his mother talking to them, his younger sisters and brothers peep out from the caravan next door. Sean and his father go out quickly to see what's wrong. Looking at his mother Sean sees tears forming in her eyes.

Holding out his hand, the garda goes to his father and tells him the bad news " We are sorry to have to tell you , your brother Mick died this morning, we received a phone call from Wales, the man who rang said he used to met you at the horse fairs, he gave his name as Horse Mick"

"I know him well" Sean's father replied, the guard continued "He said to tell you, they were having a party in a pub, they went back to the camp at closing time, Mick played the pipes till about two in the morning, he complained about pains in his chest and they got a doctor – it was too late, he died at four o clock this morning, his last request was to have the pipes sent home to your son Sean"

The travellers huddle together, frozen in their tracks.

CHAPTER 8

The Widow Lady

"Goodbye Anne".

"Goodbye Mary".

The two ladies part company after going to Mass together.

Anne lives down the road with her husband John, Mary is a widow, her husband died some years earlier from a heart attack

Mary lives alone now, except when her son Martin visits her, he is married in Ballina and calls to see her every Saturday. A religious woman of eighty seven and in good health, she goes to Mass every morning, confessions once a month, likes her own solitude.

Mary walks out of the church gates and notices the leaves are falling in the autumn breeze, it's not her favorite time of year, but then moving towards her house, she blesses herself and thinks it's good to be alive.

A slight breeze blows across the Church ground and out on to the road, the leaves are everywhere and there is a dark cloud forming overhead.

I had better get home Mary thinks, before the shower comes, moving towards her house on the hill.

She notices the birds singing has stopped as if they know there is a change coming. Passing by the graveyard she blesses herself and keeps walking.

She cannot visit Jim today, she usually calls once a week and puts flowers on the grave

Walking up the hill she notices the smoke coming out of the chimney of her house and her dog Butch glances down from the wall as if knowing the time she would arrive.

Putting the key in the door Mary says "come in Butch, its going to rain, and we'll have something to eat".

He's her only friend and a good watchdog; no one comes near the house when he's around.

Mary glances at the Sacred Heart picture in the kitchen, and thinks about her work for the day. Putting some food on a plate she leaves it on the floor for the dog, "saying good boy Butch thanks for keeping an eye on things while I was away".

Just as Mary sits down, she hears a knock on the door, the dog moves slowly towards the sound, the hair rising on his back, a jack russel, he has no fear of anything.

"Come back Butch, Mary says, it's only the Postman".

Butch recedes ever so slowly to the sound of his master, and continues to eat his food.

"It's me Mary, Tom O'Brien, I have a parcel for you, but you must sign for it".

"Hold on a minute Tom until I come to the door" answers Mary.

Mary greets the postman with a smile, saying "how are things Tom"?

"Not too bad Mary, but there is rain on the way.

She carries the parcel to the kitchen table and goes back to sign the docket

Thanks, Paddy says it must be something important.

"It is she replied, very important, closing the door

Some of these people are very nosey she says, looking down at the dog.

Between myself and the priest, what people don't know won't worry them

Finshing her tea she blesses herself and looks out the front window,

Seeing the small birds sheltering under the hedge, she throws some breadcrumbs out the window, closing it quickly from the wind and rain.

She stands at the window a few moments and glances at the grass outside, she sees her bushes and flowers losing their colour in the Autumn rain.

She smiles and thinks will I be round again to see them blooming in spring.

Returning to the table she looks at the parcel, I did not expect this today she says, but these clergymen are always in a hurry, you'd swear that the pope was going to die, but still and all, a promise is a promise.

I thought I would clean the range today, and sweep out Martin's room, himself and his wife are coming Saturday and staying for the weekend.

The local priest had told her about the parcel, but it wasn't due until the following week

Opening the parcel with a scissors, she notices a small brown envelope on top of the cloths.

Opening it, it reads "Dear Mary, Father Martin here, do the best you can with these, I enclose thread and two sets of needles, when finished, drop them down to the church, and I will collect them.

God bless you

Father Martin

Mary looks at the white vestments and thinks, "it must be busy when they sent such a big parcel".

She gets a package every month but this is the biggest so far

Mary moves back to the mantelpiece and looks at her husbands photo, smiling she picks up the small needle and thread, "I might as well get started" she says.

The white collar boy will be here next week looking for these and I'll do the best I can

I'll use my own needle and thread she thinks, what I use myself is better and stronger, that thread they sent the last time was too heavy.

She holds the white pieces of cloth up to the kitchen light, laying them down neatly on the table; she counts twelve of them, and thinks she will just have enough thread to do the job.

Mary puts her tools on the table, two needles, one spool of thread, threading the needle she smiles and thinks, it's great to have good eyesight at my age, I never needed glasses

Putting the needle through the cloth she very slowly makes the sign of the cross in red thread, holding it up to the light, she sees the red cross through the light and smiles.

Not bad she says, I have eleven more to make up and that's it for the evening.

Glancing around the kitchen, she looks at the curtains, all designed in different colours, all done by herself.

Mary was noted by the local people for her skill at knitting and sewing and many a person called to her for a cardigan or woolen hat.

What a lot of people could never understand how she had such good eyesight and never needed glasses, strange but very true.

Mary's work is disturbed by a knock on the door, who is this, she wonders.

It's raining outside and could not be a neighbour, looking out the side window she sees a dark stranger standing at the door, wet from head to toe. A tall man in dark clothes.

Finding her eyes rather sore, she rubs them and looks out through the curtains again.

The dark stranger casts his eyes towards her and Mary recognizes the man, it's her brother Jim from Manchester, she hasn't seen him for the last five years, he looks shook and frightened, his face is black from want of a shave.

As Mary moves away from the window towards the door, she notices the dog has not moved from the range, or barked at the sound of the knock.

Opening the door she sees the figure moving towards the left of the house, wondering what is wrong she says "is that you Jim, I didn't expect you today.

Moving round the back of the house she notices the bushes are moving left and right in the breeze, but her brother has disappeared.

The only sound around the house now is the church bell ringing at 12 o clock.

Mary blesses herself and says the angelus looking down at the church.

My eyes must be playing tricks on me, that's all the sewing I will do today she says, I'll have a cup of tea and a bun, the white collar man will have to wait for a while.

Looking at the dog she sees he is asleep beside the range, strange she thinks that he did not react when she opened the door.

Life is strange she thinks very strange.

Sitting down at the table she pours herself some tea, no sugar – just milk

Looking up at the photograph of her brother, she thinks it must be the weather playing tricks on her.

Mary hears the phone ringing; the dog moves his head towards the sound.

Going over Mary picks up the phone – Hello she says, who am I speaking to?

Is this Mary Dempsey the voice says?

Yes.

I am sorry to inform you, your brother had an accident last night coming from the pub.

I'm ringing from Stepping Hill hospital.

How is he Mary asks, tears forming in her eyes.

Her two hands holding the phone with fright.

He will be all right the nurse says, just a few bruises.

He was admitted to intensive care, and we will keep him there just a bit longer.

His blood pressure is a little bit high; he gave us your number and asked us to ring you

The woman that found him was a nurse and she called an ambulance, she was driving home from work last night and she noticed something moving in the dark, it was a white handkerchief, stopping her car she ran up the path towards him.

It was a handkerchief with a cross on it, your brother was unconscious, but the handkerchief had fallen from his hand, it must have been a bicycle or a scooter that knocked him down, because he fell in a bit on the kerb.

A lot of young people on scooters and bikes in the area, the police are investigating the accident.

He told me to tell you not to worry and he will contact you shortly.

Goodbye for now Mrs Dempsey

Goodbye Mary replied, sitting on the chair beside the phone, blessing herself she says "thank God he's all right".

I sent him a few of them hankies for Christmas she thinks, and a piece of the crib from the church, I told him to carry them in his pocket and they were blessed by the bishop.

Mary goes back to the table and looks at her work, the cross on the hankies look brighter now against the white cloth.

As the sun shines in the window, the clouds move away from the small house and the birds come out of their habitat, knowing that the day ahead holds the promise of warmth and sunshine before the real Autumn weather sets in.

CHAPTER 9

The Old Picture House

"Give us a PINT Mary before the bus comes"

"I will Sean, going back today are you"?

"I am surely, back to the grind on Monday"

"Never mind Sean, in a few years time you'll be home to stay, God willing".

Sean likes this old pub, Mary and himself have been friends for years. She lost her husband, Jim two years earlier, with cancer. She still runs the pub the same way as her husband.

Second generation, Sean came in here as a child, with his mother and father. In later years he used to have an orange and Mary's father would always give him two flash bars, on his way to the picture house.

"Every time I come home Mary, things are changing" Sean says, lighting a cigarette and looking up at the shelves.

"It's nice to see you still have some of the old stuff Mary, it brings back fond memories of this pub" Sean says.

"A lot of it is rubbish Sean, when the picture house closed down, the man who bought it gave me the stuff for nothing. Posters of Laurel and Hardy, Humphrey Bogart and Doris Day, they are not worth a lot Sean, but sometimes, when I'm on my own at night, I look at them on the wall and it brings back fond memories of yourself Sean and Eileen your sister, rest her soul, and myself, sixpence on a Sunday, a shilling during the week

John stands up and goes to the door, the frame of the building is still there, Sean smiles to himself when he thinks of years ago, simple times, a few sweets and a shilling. Times were hard then, his father in England at the spuds, home at Christmas, no Television, just a wireless, and a bad one at that. The Atlantic cinema was our Las Vegas, Sean smiles to himself. Those lights let us escape into our own world of fantasy, Laurel and Hardy, Roy Rogers and The Marx Brothers.

"Are you dreaming Sean"? Mary says, coming outside the counter.

"I don't know Mary, maybe I'm going daft, I'm just thinking about years ago across the road" he replies

"The picture house" she says, smiling at him.

"The picture house surely it brings back fond memories" Sean replies.

"It's closed for the last two years, a developer in Dublin bought it, he was in here last week" she replies.

"I have the keys here in the house, come on over and we'll have look inside, I am caretaker for the moment" Mary says,

"I'll take a quick look Mary; the bus will be here shortly.

Sean and Mary walk across the road, Mary puts the key in the door and lets Sean in.

"No electricity here, but there is a torch on the table, the owner is coming in a month to clear all the stuff out" she says.

John walks down the centre aisle behind Mary, its still the same old cinema, the seating has changed.

"The people who owned it had been losing money for years, Kilroys they called themselves. They also owned two cinemas in Dublin, closed now as well" Mary tells him.

Sean sits down in the front seat, looking up at the big screen.

"I always liked the pictures Mary" he says, "I still go to the odd one in London, the old films are all gone.

"Let's have a look upstairs at the balcony" says Sean.

"All right Sean, follow me"

As Sean ascends the stairs, he sees two old photographs, one of Marlyn Monroe, the other of Errol Flynn.

"These are worth something, Mary"

"Come over here Sean" Mary says "look at this poster of "Gone With The Wind". Do you remember it Sean"

"I do, it ran here for a month, some spectacle I hear, I didn't have the money at the time to go and see it. I remember seeing Ben Hur shortly afterwards, I got the money from Dad when he came from England".

Sean looks around at the old stairs, thinking about years ago, it was fantasy, simple fantasy,

"Its sad Mary" he says "all the people that came here, a few sweets and a bottle of orange, times have changed".

"They have" Mary replies, shining the torch down the stairs.

"Let's have a look at the ticket office Mary, and then we'll go"

"All right John "she answers "not a lot to see".

Mary opens the door and Sean looks around the small office, down on the ground he sees two photographs, one of Alfred Hitchcock, the other of John Wayne.

"They seem to be cut out off a newspaper" John says.

"I don't know" she replies, taking them in her hand.

"Another bit of history gone, Mary" he says.

"Don't worry John, we're still here" she answers.

"Its getting near bus time Mary, I'll have a quick one before it comes" says John.

Mary and himself walk out into the sunshine again, Sean looks up at the name over the door and smiles.

"It won't be here the next time I come home" he says

"I think not" Mary says, "this developer is going to build houses on it, but you are always welcome in my house".

The two of them walk back to the bar; Mary goes inside and pushes the glass under the optic.

"Good luck Sean" she says "it's .on the house|

"Good luck Mary. To the good old days and to the old picture house.

"Time to be going Mary, the bus is here, 'till we meet again, all the best" says Sean.

Mary hands Sean a small envelope saying "open this when you are on the bus".

"Thanks "he says, carrying his suitcase through the open door.

"Goodbye Mary and God bless you" he says, with a tear in his eye.

Sean moves up the centre aisle of the bus and sits at the very back, there are only three people on the bus. He puts the ticket in his top pocket, taking the envelope out; he wonders what can be inside, maybe the price of a drink he thinks.

Opening it he smiles, it's an old photograph of himself and Eileen and Mary standing outside the old picture house when they were very young.

The three of them smiling, eating chocolate and drinking a mineral.

Written on the bottom of the card is "Sweet memories, Mary".

John puts the picture in his inside pocket and blesses himself, thinking about his sister Eileen.

"Thanks" he says to himself, as the bus moves away from the old picture house towards the busy streets of Dublin.

CHAPTER 10

The Shoemaker

JOHNNY IS LIVING ALONE, happy in his own way, his family have left him for years.

He's happy go lucky, good neighbours, Friday in town for the pension, a few pints and a game of twenty five. Not bad, for a man of eighty five.

Sitting here on a fine day, working at his trade, he sometimes dreams of years ago when he worked in America, hard times in Chicago. He drove a taxi at night, a caddy during the day for for some of the big noises, some of them friends of Al Capone, but good men to pay – that's all that mattered.

Johnny Shoemaker they called him in Chicago, and when he returned to Ireland he was called the same by the local people. He learned his trade from a Jewboy in America, there were no machines then, just a last, rivets, a sheet of rubber and one of leather.

He brought his tools home with him, and many a tall tale was told around the fire as he carried on his trade. The only tool he bought since he returned was a sewing machine. The local hardware shop supplied the waxed thread.

Johnny liked his trade, but his eyesight was failing a bit and he had to adjust the light nearer the last.

"Are you there Johnny" a voice says outside the house

"Who's that" Johnny shouts holding his glasses down on his nose

"It's me Mick" the voice answers

"Hello Mick, come in and sit down, I\all have these shoes finished shortly" he replies "these women don't know what they want, I'll have them finished by six o clock, they belong to Mary Stenson, she works in the hospital"

"Don't hurry" Mick says "Great night in town last night, music in Flanagan's, the Guards had to clear the house".

"I Called at around ten o clock, but were in bed" Mick continues.

"I was Mick, a bit of a cold, I had a glass of the quare stuff and it did the trick, got it from a Roscommon man last week, I'll give you a drop in a minute"

Johnny takes the shoe off the last and puts up the other one.

"I'll get the bottle he says" moving towards the cupboard.

"Pull the kettle off the crane Mick, it's boiled".

He fills the two cups up halfway and puts a spoon of sugar in each of them.

"Now Mick, pour in the water, great stuff" he says

"Hard to beat it" Mick replies, tears starting to form in his eyes, with the strong taste

The two men look into the fire, Johnny smoking his pipe, Mick watching the turf show a blaze of warmth. The two men are happy in their own way. Mick is seventy five and enjoys the company of his neighbour John. Neither have a television and rely on the radio.

"Was there many musicians in the pub last night Mick" he asks

"five" Mick replies, "well, four and a bodhran player"

"Was that Finn fella there with the flute: Johnny asks, taking a puff out of his pipe.

"He was surely" Mick replies, "but he's not able to blow it like used to"

"H's getting on" John says "I knew him years ago in Chicago, a good flute player and does a small bit on the fiddle.

"I think this will be my last year at this job, Mary, my daughter wants me to move into one of the old people's houses in the town, I'm happy here.

"All the older people are moving into the town" Mick replies, drinking from the cup, :its not safe for a pensioner living on their own out the country, changed times. I won't move, I have this alarm around my neck and a button on the phone, and a gun in the corner just in case"

"I don't like the town" John says, "too many people"

"Surely John" Mick replies "the young ones roaring and shouting and taking drugs".

"Get hold of the tin whistle Mick, its on the mantelpiece, I have one shoe to finish for the Stenson one, she'll be here shortly.

I have no wind, Mick says, standing up looking at the holy picture

Just play a slow air John says, it's a pity I'm not in form, I would join you in the fiddle, my fingers ae gone a bit stiff mick

"Many a good tune we had in Flanagans years ago John saiys, hammering the rivets into the leather

Mick blows slowly on the tin whistle, playing a slow air, while John continues his work. The dog at the door moves towards the fire, while the hens outside cock their heads to the sound of music.

"Lovely Mick" says John "you are a hearty player. There is no sound of traffic only a few rabbits enjoying the evening sun, a fox stops briefly to listen, before moving on. The wind blows ever so lightly over the grass, with the flowers shining in the evening shade.

"A nice oneMick, I heard it in Chicago on Paddy's day years ago|

A knock comes to the door, a lady's voice shouts hello. John looks up and smiles – "is that you Mary" he shouts

"It is she replies"

"I will be finished in a few minutes" he replies

"She is an hour early John thinks, its six now and she wasn't supposed to be here until seven.

"Youre early" says John

|I thought if I left it any later, you might be in bed" she replies sarcastically

Bed my granny thinks, you were always too exact, that's why you never got married

"Right Mary, they are ready now" says John

Mary looks at the shoes with a frown on her face, "how much " she asks

"Two pound" says John

"Two pound for such a small job" she cries

"If you got them repaired in a shop, they would charge you a fiver just to look at them" Says John

"All right " she says, I'm in a hurry, there you are two pound" she rushes out the door talking to herself

John looks down at Mick saying, " you don't speak Mick"

"No I don't" he replies, we fell out years ago, over the medical card, she reported me to the health board, working and drawing the dole"

"She is poisin surely" John says

"If a snake bit her, the snake would die" Mick replies

"H ere Mick, hold up the cup and we"ll have another drink, and let the last day be the worst

The two old men put the cups to their mouths

"Happy days Mick John says I hope we'll be alive this time next year

" With the help of God Mick replies

I was born in this old house Mick John says

It was closed for a good few years while I was in Chicago, but I'm back now a fair while

Lighting his pipe John mutters, when my time is up I would like to die here

Don't talk about dying Mick shouts back at him, the alcochol taking affect, we are here in good health around the fire. Let the world carry on and we will drink its health

Mick puts the tin whistle to his mouth and plays a jig, the geese in the bog, John lays back on his chair looking out the small window watching the sun going down. Tapping his low boots on the concrete floor he says no more shoes today, no more shoes for that ould Stenson one he laughs.

CHAPTER 11

The Fiddle Player

IT'S A QUIET DAY in June, not much activity around the small green house, only a few thrushes on the ground, picking up what Ben the dog would not eat.

The sun is going down slowly like a ray of fire and nature is happy with the day that has gone.

The rabbits in the field enjoy the evening breeze, the cows chew the sweet grass and at the back of the house the hens move into their house for the night.

Ben, the sheepdog stands at the front door, his tongue wagging, he looks out through the small gate, showing his authority, no one enters here without his permission.

There is no fire lighting in the kitchen, Kevin the owner never lights a fire in the summertime, except maybe if he has visitors, or someone comes to play a tune.

He sits on a chair beside the hearth, thinking about the days of old, he is on his own now, all his brothers are in America and his sister Mary is in a nursing home.

Standing up he goes to the door and opens it, "It's too warm in here" he says, talking to himself, the fresh air is precious. He does not notice the birds on the lawn or see the rabbits moving in the fields across the road, he is not blind, Kevin is an albino and his sight is not great.

He smiles to himself listening to the birds singing in the evening breeze, he thinks about a jig he heard a year earlier, around this time of year, it was in the evening time Jimmy called and the two of them played the tune outside on the lawn.

Jimmy with the flute and Kevin with the fiddle, Kevin thought, after they finished playing, the birds were singing, just as they are now.

Ben looks up at his master as though he knows what he is thinking and rubs his nose along the old man's trouser leg.

The evening is disturbed by the noise of a bicycle squeaking outside the gate and the sound of a low voice.

"Hello Kevin" a voice says.

Kevin can't see him, but he knows who he is, "Hello Michael" he says "You are on the rounds again"

"I am Kevin, just heading down to Gurteen, will we have a tune"? He asks

Kevin knows the man for many years; he is a traveling musician from Foxford – Michael Towey better known as Ned, for short.

Every June he travels all over South Sligo and plays with all the musicians in the area

Kevin does not particularly like the man because he usually is looking for a drink and a bed for the night and could be hard to get rid of. Never the less, a good flute player.

The last time he stayed with Kevin, he stole a bottle of poitin off the dresser.

"Right Ned we'll have a tune" says Kevin, "But I can't offer you a bed".

"Don't worry Kevin, it's only a flying visit, if you have a drink, I'll take it, pull out two chairs on the grass and get the fiddle".

Kevin goes into the house and takes a six pack of Guinness out of the fridge.

Ned takes two wooden chairs from the kitchen and puts them along the front of the house.

"What could be better than this" Ned says. "Playing a tune on a summer's evening and the sun setting in a blaze of fire".

Kevin is not impressed by his remarks; his ears tell him things that his eyes cannot see.

"Wait until I tune up the fiddle, and we'll see how it sounds".

Kevin does not like playing with the traveling musician, because he's sometimes a bit out of tune and his music distracts Kevin.

A lot of traditional music is played in the bars, and with the large crowd of listeners a person out of tune is not always noticed.

Kevin smiles to himself, what about, Ned is getting old, lost his wife the year before, and music is all he has.

A few bottles of stout and a tune won't do a lot of harm

"Here Ned, take a drink of this"

Thanks Kevin" he says taking a drink out of the bottle, "It might soften the throat"

Ned opens his wooden case and puts the pieces of his flute together, like assembling a gun.

It's an old flute handed down to him from his grandfather, sadly, neither of his two sons have any interest in music. Ned does not care, he has held on to the instrument as though it was part of his life. When he leaves this world, it will be put in the coffin with him.

Kevin opens up his fiddle case with the same precision, adjusting the bow he rubs it with resin.

It's an old fiddle, given to him when he was twelve years old by a man from Clare called James Duffy, a man who traveled the world with his music. His friend said he foretold his own death, and he had spoken of Kevin far and wide, he said he was the only person worthy of the instrument.

Kevin held on to the fiddle like a toy and for years afterwards he would say a prayer for James and he would take the fiddle to bed with him.

Years later when he played at fleadhanna and around the pubs , some of the musicians would smile and say, Duffy is never dead while Kevin is alive.

Kevin plucks the strings to see if it's in tune, sometimes in the hot weather it goes off a bit.

"She's not so bad "he says "she will wear me out yet" as he rubs the bow over the strings.

Michael blows the flute.

The rabbits in the fields cock their ears to listen, as the birds in the trees stop singing, not disturbed , just curious about the music, as they hear the music played a few times a week.

"What will we play"? Michael asks

"We'll play Michael Prestons reel and follow it with the laurel tree", answers Kevin.

"No" Michael replies, "we won't play the laurel tree, it's a reel on its own and should stay that way.

Kevin smiles "you're right Michael, I never thought, sets of tunes run in two's or threes, but the laurel tree was always played on its own".

Michael nods in agreement and starts the reel at a very slow pace. Kevin joins him halfway through the first part, the two musicians speed things up a bit and the music seems to drift like a breeze through the bushes, down towards the bog and the stream across the road. The birds in the trees move their heads ever so slowly to the sound of the music, they were going to sleep, but now the music is a soothing sound to the end of a Summers evening.

Ducks move slowly from the river unafraid, knowing the sound of Kevins fiddle, if they could talk they would probably name the tune.

The dog lies in the still grass outside the door, looking up at his master – he has been Kevin's friend for the last ten years, the sound of the music puts a sheen on his hair in the evening sun.

The two men finish playing, both showing signs of sweat, they look at each other with tearful eyes, as if one knows what the other is thinking.

"We're not too bad yet Kevin" Michael says, rubbing his fingers with his tongue.

"No we're not" Kevin replies, giving his bow a rub of resin.

The two men know each other a long time, and they have fallen out a few times, it nearly came to blows over at a fleadh in County Roscommon but they made it up again.

It was all over the name of a tune that Michael Coleman composed, one said the name was "The Kilavil Polka" and the other insisted it was "The traveling Postman".

A man called Dempsey from Balla said what about "What difference does it make, as long as the two of you can play it and it sounds good".

Kevin opens a bottle of guinness and hands it to Michael.

"Thanks" he says "We'll play two more reels and then I'll be on my way".

"All right" Kevin agrees "What will we play"?

"We'll we play two of Coleman's, – The Sunny Banks and Mammy's Pet" says Michael.

It's only fitting since I'm in his county that I show him some respect

"All right" Kevin says "start it off and I'll follow".

Kevin thinks to himself, you had a shot or two of the quare stuff between here and Foxford my boy, but you won't get any of mine.

My eyesight is not too good, he thinks, but that's the sort of talk he was going on with in Gurteen after Poitin a few years earlier.

Michael looks over at his partner and smiles, "You wouldn't have a drop of the white stuff"? He asks.

"You'll get no white stuff here" Kevin replies "You have to cycle in to Gurteen yet, if that stuff hits you'll have to be carried in.

"A small drop Kevin, it softens the tone of the flute, and it gives the bones a bit of oil to keep going"

"All right Michael, you'd better get moving, it's getting dark and Gurteen is another five miles.

Kevin goes out to the well at the side of the house and pulls on piece of rope, he hides it here all the time, what people don't know won't worry them he thinks.

Pulling up the bucket from the well, Michael comes around the side of the house, hearing the sound, Kevin shouts at him to go back.

"I'll give you a drop in a cup and you'll have to go, it's getting late"

Washing a cup in the bucket, he takes the bottle of poitin and unties it, he always ties it through the handles, its his own secret and sometimes on a frosty morning when he comes to the well, a shot of the quare stuff with hot water gives him a great lift.

Holding the bottle at an angle he fills the cup to the top and takes a drink himself.

"Now Michael" he says "that's your drink for the road until we meet again".

"Thanks Kevin" Michael says with glee in his eyes "We'll play one more tune and we'll call it a day".

"All right lad, but remember it's the last one for the road" answers Kevin in a stern voice.

"We'll play "The ten penny bit" by Paddy Killoran, Michael, and then we'll pack it up for the night.

The two musicians start their music with precision, you'd think it was their last tune together, but to the two men sitting in the evening shade, there is a bond that will never be broken, they may argue and fall out, but when it comes to playing together, God himself could not separate them.

The flowers along the house seemed to have changed colour with the twilight creeping in, and the birds are ready to sleep as if they know the concert is over, even the dog moves in to the kitchen and sits beside his master's chair.

The music finishes on the last bow of Kevin's fiddle, and the two men put their instruments away.

Kevin goes into the kitchen and puts the case under the bed, looking up at the Sacred Heart picture he blesses himself and gives thanks. Walking to the door he sees Michael tying his case to the carrier of the bike.

"Look after yourself Michael" Kevin says, "Stay on the road".

"I will" Michael says "I might make Gurteen before closing time".

"All right Kevin smiles "I'll see you next year, either here or beyond".

"Don't be talking like that Kevin" he replies, "The man above wants us to stay here for another while; them boys up there have no interest in our music".

"Be off with you" Kevin says, "and don't drink too much".

Kevin goes back to the house, smiling, turning on the light he thinks Michael is going a bit daft like himself.

Looking at Ben in the corner, he says "I forgot to put the bottle back in the well"

Going around the back of the house he looks for the bottle he left on the wall – "It's gone" he gasps "It's gone, you stole my fuckin' bottle Murphy".

Kevin returns to the house, talking to himself, "That's the last tune you'll play here" he says, "and that's for sure".

Kevin slams the door behind him and looks at his fiddle under the bed saying "Its just you and me now my man, just you and me, there will be no more music in this house from anyone else".

Kevin sits on the chair beside his dog and smiles, saying "I said it before, but what's the point, every time someone calls with a flute or a fiddle, the music takes over the mind and all anger and resentment is forgotten about"

Kevin rubs his dog and thinks you can't win.

Nodding his head he goes to sleep and dreams of music and fleadheanna.

The musician is asleep, tomorrow he will awaken to a brighter day and you never know who might call for a tune with the white headed fiddle player.

CHAPTER **12**

The Blacksmith

IT'S A SUMMERS EVENING in June, the sun is nesting slowly, in a sea of red, it has done its job for today, and man & nature are happy with the day that has passed.

Paddy looks out of his shed towards his house and rubs his forehead with his hand "thank God that its got a bit cooler" he says, talking to himself. The hens walking beside the shed are not disturbed by Paddy waving his big hammer on the anvil; neither do the crows fly away with the loud noise.

Paddy is a blacksmith, probably one of the few left in Co Leitrim, the skills of his trade are still well known in the area.

He has been shoeing horses for the last fifty years, like his father before him. He knows with the march of time that his trade is coming to an end, only Michael up the road, and Jim Rooney have horses now, and they are mostly for show.

Looking at Paddy's old shed it would be hard to count all the horses that have passed through here, some for royalty, some for ploughing, and even the travelers called here looking for advice about horses.

Not only is Paddy a blacksmith, he is also a man who has grown up with horses, in his childhood his grandfather kept some jumpers, and from a very early age Paddy was taught the tricks of the trade, how to buy, how to sell, how to treat sickness and injuries with natural cures, all learned at a young age and never forgotten.

Paddy is old now, in his seventies, his trade is mostly sleans, fire tongs, shovel heads, the day of the horse is near an end and the only reminder Paddy has of the old days is his old horse" Polly" a

Clydesdale, Paddy bought her from a dealer in Mayo, a good animal, and a fine specimen of excellent breeding.

With Polly walking around the building, he feels he can still hold on to a part of the past that is fast disappearing. But there is a frown on Paddy's face this last few months, he knows that his trade is coming to an end, and he will soon have to retire.

The building he is working in is in bad shape/ it has been condemned by the local council, seemingly some of the people in the area feel that it is in a dangerous condition so near the main road. The local council offered him an alternative place but Paddy has been here a long time and he will not move, even if they knock the forge down.

Paddy will not leave his home not for anyone.

His father died here and his grandfather. If Paddy is going to go, he will be carried out in a box.

Mary walks into the forge, a robust woman of sixty five.

She married Paddy forty years ago, they have two children, and both are overseas. Jim is an accountant in America and Mary, a pharmacist in England

Paddy and Mary worked hard to educate the family, Paddy at his blacksmiths trade while Mary worked for the local doctor and his wife, minding the kids and doing general housework, both now happy in their retirement, living at one with nature. a horse in the yard, chickens in the coup and a few hen pheasants in a pen at the back of the house.

Mary looks at her husband and thinks if they knock the forge, it will kill Paddy, his strong arms his hardy features, his keen eye for horseshoeing, take this away from Paddy and you take his heart away.

His life as a blacksmith is in his blood, his body and mind never knew anything else, horses are part of his life, a gift from the man above, proven time and time again, even the local vet, a Scottish bloke often called to Paddy for advice about a mare or a foal who might be sick.

Paddy looks over at his wife standing in the doorway,

"You're getting old Mary, no more than me" he says, "still, we have our health thank God and maybe when this engineer calls next week he might change his mind"

Even though Paddy knows his horseshoeing days are over, he still tries to look at the positive side of life and is grateful to be able to knock around and be at peace with himself and those around him.

"Come on" Mary says "your dinner is ready for the last hour, so call it a day.

"I will Mary, wait till I put my tools away". Paddy puts his shoeing hammer in a small box, cleaning both it and wiping off the anvil.

He walks out of his workshop into the yard, putting both bolts on the door.

He stands back and looks at the building, it's gone a bit rough with the march of time he thinks, but it could tell a story or two.

I had better stop dreaming he says, talking to himself, and go and have the bacon and cabbage.

Walking into the kitchen he looks over at his wife standing at the big range which has been falling to pieces lately, he has recently done some work on it and now it seems to be pulling ok.

He smiles, looking at his wife he says "Mary the range is working better than the two of us now"

"Speak for yourself she replies, this old thing should be thrown out years ago".

"I suppose its part of the furniture round here" she replies "it will do its job for the length we want it".

"Did the post come yet Mary"? Paddy asks

"It did surely, but I didn't open it yet"

Going over to the table she picks the letters up and hands them to him, Paddy leaves them on the window saying "I'll have the feed first, and then I'll open them".

Looking out the window at the evening sunset, Paddy sits at the big brown table and Mary leaves the food in front of him, boiled spuds, lean bacon, cabbage and onions.

Paddy's dog "Butch" having smelled the food is pawing at the door.

"Hump off" Mary shouts, "You'll have yours when we finish ours"

Sitting down to her dinner across from Paddy, she blesses herself and says "thank you God for the day that is gone and for the food that we are about to eat".

"Amen" Paddy says

The two people peel the potatoes with precision and each watches the other enjoying their food

There was never a whole pile of money in the house but there was plenty of food, bacon and meat in the fridge, a good vegetable garden at the back of the house and plenty of free range eggs to go with it

"Turn on the radio and we'll hear the news" he says,

"Wait till we finish our food" his wife replies, "Sure what's on it only bad news"

You're a queer one Mary he thinks, awful bossy set in her ways, even the television is not switched on for weeks, except for a football match or the horse show.

Both enjoy a similar lifestyle away from the busy world.

Mary reads her books from the library most nights, and Paddy fixes the odd collar for the horses.

When Mary goes to bed Paddy goes back to the cupboard and pulls out a book about horses, it was written by a Plains Indian on a reservation in North America.

A yank on holidays a few years earlier visited Paddy in his forge and Paddy gave him a present of a saddle, just because he liked the man.

The two of them chatted for hours about horses, right into the early morning. This man kept horses in America, his mother descended from an Indian tribe, whose name Paddy could not remember.

The man promised Paddy he would send him a book when he returned home, he said it contained natural cures known only to the Indians.

Paddy looks at his wife sleeping on the chair "I'll have a quick read before she wakes up.

He always keeps the book well hidden from the wife, just in case she might lose it.

Paddy gets up ever so slowly from the chair and going towards the cupboard he notices the letters on the window, picking them up he sees one with no stamp, this is the one he thinks, the one I didn't want to get.

Opening it he puts on his reading glasses, Dept of Environment etc he reads,

Dear Sir

We wish to inform you, the building known as the forge is in a dangerous state and may be condemned by the local council.

An Engineer will call to you next week on Thursday 20 June at 4 pm and he will make a final decision as to the state of the building.

His decision is final and no further appeals will be accepted.

If he decides your building is in a dangerous state, he will have no choice but to issue a condemnation order for its demolition

Holding you in readiness

Yours faithfully

Mary Smith – Local Environmental Officer

Paddy fires the letter on the table, accidentally knocking over a cup, breaking it.

The noise wakes his wife "what's the matter Paddy, have you lost your brains".

"Read that" he shouts back at her.

"Give me your glasses" she says, rubbing her eyes

Mary studies the letter saying "it looks bad all right, it's a week away we'll just have to wait and see"

"Wait and see!" Paddy shouts "this buck is coming next Thursday; I'll hit him with the hammer if he condemns this place"

"He can't shift us out of the house" she says.

"If he knocks that building Mary" he says, "I won't wait in this place, I'll move up the mountain and live in a caravan".

"Take it easy Paddy" Mary says "something will turn up and you never know, the engineer may not be that bad".

Mary looks up at Paddy and thinks, its over for the two of us; we'll just have to move elsewhere.

"If they shift us they will have to compensate us" Mary says.

"Where will we go to"? She says, before Paddy can open his mouth.

Their argument is interrupted by the dog barking and a loud knock on the door.

"Are you there Paddy" a voice shouts,

A man in his fifties comes through the door, panting.

Paddy looks at him anxiously, "what's wrong with you Jim, have you seen a ghost"?

"Give me a drink of water quick" he replies, "I'm after running two miles".

"Here" Mary says, "drink this, handing him a pint of milk off the table".

"What's wrong?" she asks "is the wife sick, or was there an accident"?

Jim McGowan or Jimmy G as they call him, drinks the milk and sits down on the chair, saying "that's better".

There's been an accident up at Biddy's gap, a man and his wife and son went off the road in their jeep, they are trapped inside, I tried the tractor, but it's no use"

"The young lad may have broken his leg and we can't get him out of the jeep, the tractor keeps skidding, its very boggy there Paddy".

Paddy knows the place, several people got stuck there, but this fellow must have gone in too far.

"How did he get in so far?" Paddy asks, "he should have turned back".

"I don't know Paddy", he replies, but he has this big jeep, he probably thought it couldn't happen with the machine he has.

"You've tried to get him out"? Paddy asks

"I have", Jim replies, but the tractor keeps skidding and the driver and his family are jammed in a corner bank, and can't open the doors.

Paddy looks at Mary, "we'll have to try Polly" he says, "he might move it a bit, myself and Jim will try to dig some of the mud away".

"Mary, you'll have to come with us, its not totally dark yet, but this job will take time, no ambulance will get up that road".

"Hurry up" Mary shouts, "We haven't got all day".

"I'll open the forge, and you get Polly, he will be a bit nervous, he has not pulled a cart in ages but it's the only chance of getting them back here if they are hurt".

"Jim, you go back to the gap" she says "Myself and Paddy will be there shortly, and here, bring the torch".

Paddy looks at the clock, "its nine o clock Mary, and we'd better hurry.

"Get Polly tackled up and the two of us will back him into the cart" she shouts.

Paddy moves out into the yard towards the barn.

Mary follows him out, pulling a scarf over her head.

"It's not going to rain" Paddy says, wondering what she wants the scarf for,

"It's not the rain she says, it's the midges, and don't be so smart" she says, giving him a dirty look.

Paddy puts the bit in the horses mouth and Mary moves some of the tools away from the cart, its years since we used this she thinks, but we'll go up that bog road, with Polly pulling it, and maybe a bit of a shove.

Paddy and Mary move out of the yard onto the main road, Polly is not too happy with his load, but he has done this before and he knows his master will not push him too hard.

Paddy sits on the cart slowly moving the reins, he might not have done this for years, but once learned, never forgotten.

Smiling at Mary beside him, he thinks about the two of them, years ago, going to the bog.

"It will be dark by the time we get to the gap" Mary says, "I just hope Polly doesn't get stuck".

"He won't", Paddy replies, taking a side road, up by Tom Ryan's and turning left at the river.

"No car has traveled here for years Mary" but I have walked Polly up there several times, we'll come in just at the back of the gap.

"You have the hay rope"? Mary asks.

"I have" he replied.

"We'll get them out, but someone else will have to move the machine, it's a very deep hole, I hope they are not badly hurt.

Paddy moves the horse to the left up a side road, the rabbits move aside and a badger cocks his head at the sound of the voices.

No one ever comes up this road only a stray cow or a donkey.

Its getting dark as Paddy moves his cargo across the shallow river on to the narrow road.

Polly keeps her head above the whins and bushes, she knows the road.

Seeing a light in the distance, Paddy gives the reins to his wife and jumps off the cart, slowly dragging Polly to the head of the road.

"Are you there Jim" he shouts,

"I am" Paddy he replies, "I thought you would take the other road" he says

"I'm here now Jim, and that will do" Paddy shouts.

Going to the top of the small hill he shines the torch down on the jeep and sees they are badly stuck.

"Paddy, throw me down the rope off the cart" Jim shouts "and I'll tie it to the door, then we'll shovel some of the muck away and give the horse a chance".

"Are you all right in there" Paddy shouts.

The driver answers "we cannot open the windows and the doors are jammed"

"These bloody modern jeeps" Paddy says, "the windows are probably automatic and we will have to force the lock to get them out, Mary hand me down the torch, shining the light on the back door, he sees its open a small bit.

"Thank God" he says, "now if I can tie the rope around it, it will probably open with a pull from the right".

Mary slides down the bank with the torch and Jim follows.

Its dark now and only the torch lights up the night.

"Anybody hurt" Paddy enquires,

"My wife is in shock and our young son's leg is badly injured" the driver replies.

"Don't worry; we'll have you out of there shortly" Paddy replies.

Tying one end of the rope around the back door, Paddy climbs up the bank with the other end.

Polly stands motionless in the faint moonlight as Paddy ties the rope to the horse's collar.

"Come on Polly" he shouts, "we'll have to shift the door or those people will never get out.

Polly moves ever so slowly as the door of the jeep breaks open on to the soft ground.

"Hold up Polly"! He shouts – well done, clapping the horse on the back.

Mary shines the torch into the jeep, "Hand me out the child" she says, "then, the two of you can follow".

The man hands the young boy to Mary. Smiling, she says "Don't be worried young fellow; we'll have you home in no time".

The young lad grabs hold of Mary, shaking and crying.

"Here Jim" she shouts, "hand him up to Paddy".

Jim takes the child, wrapping his jacket around him, handing him over to Paddy at the horse and cart, he ventures down the trench again.

"All right" Jim calls out, the lady first, then, yourself.

The lady climbs out the back door and Mary holds her hand, guiding her out of the hole, while Jim helps the driver.

"My leg is hurt" the driver says, "all right" Jim says, we'll try to help you up"

Paddy reaches down with rope again and slowly guides the horse forward.

"Thank you" the man replies, lying down on the ground.

"The three of you can travel on the cart; I have a few coats here to wrap up the young lad. Come on Polly its time to go home" Paddy says.

"You keep the light Jim, and ring an ambulance from Maguire's house. Tell them to call at the forge"

Jim rushes through the heather towards Maguire's, shouting back at Paddy "I'll be as fast as I can".

The three patients sit on the back of the cart shivering.

Paddy says "Don't worry we'll be home shortly, and Mary will have some hot soup made up in no time".

Paddy glances down at his wife, smiling; she is black from head to toe, "Stop your grinning" she says "and start moving".

"You look like something out of the Black and White Minstrel show with all that mud on your face" Paddy says.

Mary sits upon the cart beside him, glancing back at the patients, she puts her hands around the young lad saying "pull that jacket around you, we'll be home shortly".

Paddy backs the cart up and turns the horse for home.

Its five o clock in the morning now and the sun is just lifting its head over the mountain, the heather moves lightly in the cool morning breeze, as if saying goodbye to its visitors.

The badger stares at the strangers as they move towards civilization.

The ambulance is waiting at Paddy's place when they arrive; some of the local people arrive, enquiring if Paddy or Mary is sick. When they see the two of them trotting up the road in the horse and cart, with three people on the back, they are dumbfounded.

This will be on the paper next week, one person says, it will surely another replies.

It did appear on the paper, it read "Tourists saved by blacksmith with his horse and cart", it was the talk of the area for months afterwards.

Two weeks after the escapade Paddy goes out to the yard, looking at his workshop he says" I wont open it, wait till this boy calls, then we'll see what happens.

Going back to the kitchen he sees Mary sitting down, crying.

"It's all over Paddy" she says "this engineer will condemn it, and we'll probably have to find different lodgings"

"Don't worry Mary; if it does happen, we won't be put out on the road, the house is all right, it's the shed that is causing the problem"

Paddy says reassuringly.

Paddy hands her a handkerchief "dry your eyes now and we'll have two mugs of strong tea".

Just as Paddy is wetting the tea, a jeep pulls into the yard.

"Let him wait until we finish our tea, then we will talk to him"

Paddy watches him through the kitchen window, as he climbs out of the jeep, he pulls a briefcase out and opens it, he is wearing sunglasses.

He walks over to the forge, seeing it is locked, he goes back to the jeep and makes a phone call.

Paddy walks out to the yard bringing his mug with him, and says "hello, can I help you"?

The man looks over at the building and says "I have come to inspect the forge; I have an inspection order from the County Council".

Paddy cannot see the man's face because he is looking away from him.

Gong over to the shed Paddy takes off the lock and opens the door.

The man walks in, inspecting the building; looking at the anvil and hammer he says "you keep your tools in good condition".

"I do" Paddy replies "I have been using them a long time".

The man turns to face Paddy, "how is the horse"? he asks

Paddy stands motionless; looking at his face.

"Jesus Christ" he says "you're the man we pulled out of Biddy's gap two weeks ago".

The man removes his glasses and smiles, slight bruises showing under his eyes.

Shaking hands with Paddy he says "bring out your wife I want to talk to her".

Mary walks into the shed, trying to cover the tears in her eyes with the hanky.

Looking at Paddy she asks "when do we move"?

"I don't know" Paddy says, "do you know this fellow"?

Mary throws an ugly glance at the man, then she walks over to him, staring "you're the man from the gap" she says. Her hand shaking drying her tears.

"You're not the engineer" she asks

"I am" the man replies, "I was up here on holidays at the time of the accident" shaking her hand.

"My name is John Williams and it is my job to assess the condition of the building, I'm not going to condemn this place, but you'll have to carry out some restoration Paddy".

"You'll have to put new galvanize on the roof, no tourist will be allowed to enter the workshop, and you'll have to put a gate three feet out from the shed saying no admittance. If you comply with these recommendations, there will be no problem. Do you understand Paddy"? asks the man

"I do" Paddy replies, still suffering from shock.

"All right Paddy, you have six months to carry out this work, and then there will be another inspection".

Shaking Paddy's hand he moves back to the jeep, opening the door he puts his hand under the seat and pulls out a parcel.

"This is for you from my wife, and this is yours Paddy" reaching for a bottle of brandy from the dash.

Putting his hand in his pocket he pulls out a bag of jelly beans, for the horse.

Sitting in the drivers seat, he closes the door, shouting out the window "Adios Paddy till we meet again"

Paddy waves goodbye to the man as he leaves the yard, locking the shed door, himself and his wife go back to the house, both speechless after the experience.

"Well Mary, strange how things happen" ventures Paddy

"Its not strange at all" she says "it's a bloody miracle, I was praying all week for a miracle and there it is".

Paddy sits down in the chair, laughing, Mary goes over to the range and blesses herself.

"We have a bit of work to do Paddy" she says.

"We have Mary, we have, but its better than thinking the worst.

Mary hands him a mug of tea and sits down beside him smiling.

"It's good to be alive Paddy on such a fine day".

"It is surely" he says "watching the sun shining in the window".

The two of them walk out into the yard and look at the blacksmiths shed. Old battered and in need of repair but with the sun shining on it still holds a little bit of heaven.

CHAPTER 13
The Old School

JOHN LOOKS AT HIS parent's tombstone, Mary & John Regan, they are dead a long time he thinks.

He blesses himself and says a prayer, its John's first time back in twenty years.

He was born in this area and since his mother and father died, he has not returned home.

He received a letter some months ago about a school reunion and thinking about his schooldays he decided to visit home.

John has lived in New York for a long time, a busy city and the only Irish connection he has over there are a few Irish friends and his music.

He plays the accordion – he had a good night last night in the hotel, bodhrans, fiddles and flutes, but, today he must return to the smoke. The plane leaves Shannon at four o clock.

Looking across the stoneware he thinks a lot of his friends are buried here, as he glances towards the wall he sees the roof of a building shaded by large trees, it still stands out in the morning sunshine.

The old school, John thinks, leaving the graveyard he drives right in the direction of the building, it's a bad road and nobody ever comes up here anymore.

Parking the car beside the old road. I will walk from here he thinks, no point getting stuck in the mud

Walking up, he looks at his watch, its ten o clock; I won't have much time for looking around he thinks to himself.

John looks at the bushes and trees along the road and thinks about his own schooldays, himself Willie Clancy and Michael Scally, walking home in the evening.

This was a busy road then, he thinks, every one carrying a satchel

He met a lot of them at the reunion last night, and some of them he will never see again

John takes out his hankie as he nears the wall of the old school; its ghostly shape shines out in the summer sunshine, windows broken, doors gone. But it still holds its character of years ago

Modern times have changed everything, but the old School stands proud, even with the march of time.

There is a gate in the opening; the wall is breaking apart.

Standing at the opening John looks at the building, its now a home to cattle and sheep, smiling he thinks, funny looking students, standing around the place, and not too many public conveniences, walking up to the entrance, he reads the inscription"Scoil Nasiunta"

The date is gone, two birds fly out of the broken window as he enters the large room, there is nothing left now, only the four walls, all the floorboards are broken, and except for the large blackboard it has lost all its character, it stands hidden in the corner, its shadow shining across the dark room.

Looking around the room he sees an old desk in the corner beside the stove, John walks over to it and thinKs this is the desk Himself and Willie Clancy sat in years ago, poor Willie he died four years ago from cancer, he said a prayer for him in the graveyard today, just before he visited his parents grave.

John looks down at the desk and wipes a tear from his eye, poor old Willie, we kept in contact for years, a dear old friend.

He heard about his death in America, but the poor man was dead and buried before he knew anything about it. John blesses himself and dries his eyes with the hankie

The silence in the room is broken by the sound of a voice over at the entrance,

Who's there a voice says. Then in a louder voice John hears a second voice saying, are you lost.

Looking over at the doorway he sees two shadows by the school door, walking back slowly, he notices two girls holding hands as if afraid to enter the room.

"What are your names"? John asks, watching the girls holding hands at the doorway.

"My name is Mary and this is my sister Patricia, we were just out for a walk" she says, "and we thought we heard a noise from the school".

John smiles at the girls saying,

"I was probably talking to myself, I went to school here years ago,

"Are ye from around here"? He asks

"We are", the tallest girl replies.

"We live just up the field with our Mother, Mary Clancy. Our father died some years ago.

We had a Mass for him this morning".

John holds out his hand to the two girls, saying "come in here and I'll show you something".

The two girls walk slowly in to the schoolroom staring at John with suspicious eyes.

"I went to school with your father" John says; "he and I were good friends, the two of us sat at this desk for years, and many a caning we got from the master Mr. Griffin".

"John Regan is my name, and I'm home from America on holidays, I didn't meet your mother at the reunion, did she not go"? He asks.

"No" Mary replies, "she does not socialize much, since Dad died she doesn't go out very often".

"This place is not much now", John says, "but your father and I had some happy days here".

"Tell your mother that you were talking to me – here is my card with my address, you might ask her to post on a photograph of your father.". The small girl takes the card, saying thanks.

"Our father used to take us here for walks when we were younger she says,

We would come here on a summers evening and he would talk about his young days at the school.

He mentioned that he sat at that desk with a dear old friend – he never mentioned the name".

John looks down at the school desk and tries to holds the tears back, poor old Willie he thinks, we were good buddies.

Going back to the girls he puts his arms around them, crying.

"God bless you, and the man that is gone".

Walking out the school door he notices that it has gone dark, rain on the way he thinks.

"I have to be moving now ladies" he says, "tell your mother to write to me, wont you," he says.

The tall girl says "you are welcome to come up to the house and have some tea".

"Sorry" John replies, "I have a plane to catch, I'd better be moving, but the next time I come I'll make it a date".

Moving out the gate he looks back at the school and waves goodbye to the two girls.

Looking up the road he thinks times have changed, a slight breeze seems to push the trees to one side, as if saying goodbye to their pupil.

John walks up the lane towards his car, looking back at the building, he notices the girls have gone, until we meet again Willie, he says, blessing himself, "Good luck and mind that school desk. I want to see it again the next time I come home'.

There is a noise in the schoolroom, a slight breeze seems to whistle through the broken glass, just for a moment, a ray of sunshine shines on the school desk, then disappears to a shadow as if it was being watched by somebody.

It's getting dark now and the sounds of nature are taking over, both inside and outside the old building.

The character of the building still holds its own even among its untamed friends.

Who knows, maybe they too, are pupil's of the old school.

ISBN 142515826-9

Edwards Brothers Malloy
Oxnard, CA USA
September 8, 2015